SU

The dry Martian soil was more treacherous than they thought.

As Nathan, Alice, and Karl fanned out to check out the fallen parachute, the ground became an obstacle course of sharp red rocks, hidden cracks, and deep gullies. Stumbling more than once, Nathan was ready to warn his teammates to be super careful, but decided not to start acting like some nerdy scoutmaster. Alice and Karl could take care of themselves.

Suddenly, he saw a puff of red dust and heard a yell over his helmet radio link. Scanning the area for his friends, he saw only Karl.

Alice had disappeared from the face of Mars . . .

## THE YOUNG ASTRONAUTS

## CATCH THE ADVENTURES
## FROM THE VERY BEGINNING!!

#1:  THE YOUNG ASTRONAUTS          (3002-2, $2.95)

#2:  READY FOR BLASTOFF            (3173-4, $2.95)

#3:  SPACE BLAZERS                 (3178-5, $2.95)

#4:  DESTINATION MARS              (3307-9, $2.95)

And coming in April:

THE YOUNG ASTRONAUTS #6: CITIZENS OF MARS

*Available wherever paperbacks are sold, or order direct from the Publisher. Send cover price plus 50¢ per copy for mailing and handling to Zebra Books, Dept. 3307, 475 Park Avenue South, New York, N.Y. 10016. Residents of New York, New Jersey and Pennsylvania must include sales tax. DO NOT SEND CASH.*

# The YOUNG ASTRONAUTS

## #5 SPACE PIONEERS

**RICK NORTH**

**ZEBRA BOOKS**
**KENSINGTON PUBLISHING CORP.**

ZEBRA BOOKS

are published by

Kensington Publishing Corp.
475 Park Avenue South
New York, NY 10016

First printing: March, 1991

Printed in the United States of America

*To Arthur Byron Cover*
*for pointing me in the right direction.*

# Chapter One

"Now there are Martians!"

The words kept ringing in Nathan Long's ears. After all the seven months and millions of miles, they had finally achieved the biggest milestone to date. They had landed on Mars. Dr. Allen, the adult leader of their mission, had spoken no more than the truth. *They* were the Martians.

But now, their greatest challenge was about to begin.

"Nathan! Snap out of it!"

"Huh?" said Nathan. "Wha—oh." His best friend, Sergei Chuvakin, was looking down at him with his hands on his hips. Sergei's gaze, which usually looked like it had been chipped from the clear blue ice at the heart of a glacier, was open and concerned, if a little frustrated. Nathan shook his head, trying to dislodge the wool from his mind. "I guess I was doing it again, huh?"

Sergei shook his own head. "My friend, you are

developing a habit of worrying too much. You are getting very good at it, too."

"But just think of everything there is to do — everything that could go wrong. I—"

"If you don't watch out," said another voice, "you're going to wake up and find out you've turned into an adult."

"Fat chance of that ever happening to you," Nathan told him. "You were born a menace to society and you've been trying to live up to that image ever since."

Gen Akamasu just grinned back at him. They had all removed the helmets from their pressure suits after the safe landing. They still were wearing the rest of their outfits, though, while the post-landing check for any slow leaks or other damage to the ship was being completed. All of them, that is, except for Gen. Gen's space suit was already hanging in its rack and Gen himself was wearing only the red one-piece coveralls that were standard-issue aboard the Santa Maria. Even that was open almost to his waist. Underneath it was a heavy-metal T-shirt showing a guitar with fins like a cartoon rocket that was shedding lightning bolts off into space. Nathan had never seen the shirt before.

Sergei was squinting at Gen, too. "Is that a new shirt?"

"*Someone* has to set the style on Mars," said Gen. "I don't see anyone here whose taste is better than mine, so—"

"A pretty weak accomplishment if you ask me," Alice Thorne told him from her seat at Nathan's left.

Gen flung one hand dramatically over his chest and looked up at the heavens. "Wounded by the reviews!" he said. "But what do you expect from a New Zealand sheep-farmer anyway?"

"Herder," said Alice, with a tone of mock warning.

Lanie Rizzo directed her own grin at Gen. Lanie's expression, perfected in her life on the big-city streets of Chicago, had enough sneer and enough growl in it to stop you in your tracks. If you weren't a friend of hers, that is. "Well, I think it's *cute.*"

Gen kept his smile, but now it was clearly pained. He hated to be called cute, and Lanie knew it. There wasn't much the seven of them in Nathan's team didn't know about each other, after Houston, spending almost every day with each other the *Icarus* station in Earth-orbit and the *Santa Maria* all the way to Mars. "Where did you stash that thing all this time, anyway?" Lanie added.

Gen looked back at the ceiling. "I'll never tell."

"It could have been worse," Sergei commented. "He could have been selling autographs." Sergei, a native of Leningrad, had the slightly prim attitude toward capitalism and the free enterprise system shared by many modern Russians, even after the collapse of communism and the striking social

9

changes in their own country.

Gen stared at Sergei. "Now *that,*" Gen said, is an interesting idea."

*Santa Maria* had landed on the surface of Mars only an hour or so before, the last ship of the convoy to touch down. *Niña* and *Pinta* had come down ahead of them in their designated sites straggling off to the west and were reporting that their own checkouts said everything was fine. All three ships were still on alert status until every significant detail had been verified, which was the reason their passengers were still hanging around in their pressure suits, trying to work off the nervous tension of the approach to the planet and the landing.

At least they'd been able to pack away the safety harnesses that had suspended them along the corridors during the descent. By common agreement, most everyone on *Santa Maria* who wasn't on duty with a pressing job to do had congregated in the ship's hub; after all, it was not only the physical center of the ship but the social center as well. The Hub Cafe over at the other side of the area was still packed. No one had eaten before or during the descent, of course, and a serious epidemic of munchies had set in as soon as they'd hit the ground.

In another area of the rec room was the gym. As the ship had neared Mars, people had gotten more serious about hitting the exercise machines and trying to get themselves in tone. By the time they reached Mars they would have been traveling in zero-g, without gravity, for over half a year. When you added the additional time they'd spent on the *Icarus* space station in orbit around Earth, they'd passed the better part of a year in weightlessness. Even with the facilities of the gym the weightless environment had taken its toll. Weightlessness wasn't a free ride. Over an extended period without gravity, the heart and other muscles grew weaker without the tone required to resist gravity's constant pull, the immune system, and one's ability to fight illness declined, and bones became brittle. Now they were back in gravity's domain. True, gravity on Mars was only .38 times as great as that on Earth, but it was a whole lot healthier than no gravity at all. Most people would be exhausted for days. The work rosters wouldn't push them hard for a while, giving everyone frequent sit-down breaks and limited shifts of heavy labor. Nathan wasn't looking forward to it. Just being on his feet and walking around since the landing had taken a lot out of him.

Not all of them had been hit equally, though. Nathan liked Alice a lot, but she was almost disgustingly spry and chipper at the moment. Of course, Alice had spent an awful lot of time in the one place on *Santa Maria* that *had* had gravity during the trip, or at least artificial-gravity. The agronomy section with its banks of hydroponic plant basins stretched all the way around the deck of a special compartment designed to spin while the ship was in flight. The centrifugal force created by this rotation made people on the floor of the compartment feel the same gravity as the surface of Mars.

The biology section centrifuge had been permanently stopped before they'd started the landing sequence. Now, the long cylindrical floor that had been "down" during the trip was a constant vertical wall around a large open room. The tanks and equipment on the "floor" were designed to pivot around for landing. Soon, though, Alice and the other agronomy specialists would get to work converting the section for the needs they now faced. Even that conversion wouldn't be permanent. Once their situation on Mars had been stabilized, *Santa Maria* herself would be dismantled and incorporated into the base, and the plants would make the move to a new greenhouse on the surface.

So much to do! But the expedition had the people for it. On the voyage from Earth, Nathan's original seven-person team had gotten to know and be comfortable with a much wider group of friends. Over there with Lanie was Tara White, the girl from New York City, and across the floor from them Nathan could see Lisette getting her own team into shape. As if she could feel his gaze, the dark-haired French-Canadian turned her head in Nathan's direction and gave him a smile and a quick wave. Nathan grinned back. He could hardly believe that he and Lisette were an item, but they were.

Someone from his team hadn't spoken up, Nathan realized. Noemi. The six of them had grabbed a spot together down toward the back of The Commons. That had originally been Gen's name for, well . . . the rest of the rec area that wasn't gym or commissary, but like so many things Gen came up with, the name had immediately caught on around the ship. Gen was a natural-born trend-setter. Next to them on the wall was the bank of monitors that showed them the flight deck and trajectory readouts.

They had arrived at the place they'd dedicated themselves to reach for years — the surface of Mars. The three ships and everyone on them were safe. So why did Noemi look so concerned?

"Noemi?" Nathan said.

He had to ask again, since he didn't want to attract everyone else's attention away from the good time they were having. All of them were like fish out of water, in a very literal sense, Nathan reminded himself ruefully, but Noemi Velasquez in many ways had had the roughest time of any of them. There'd been no place to shop for millions of miles, no place to see and be seen, and charm and vivacity were not necessarily the best tools for facing a hostile universe. Was it hitting her again?

Noemi's attention was glued to the monitor, to the trajectory readout of one of the cargo probes showing on the right of the split screen. She hadn't freaked out. She could almost do the mathematics behind orbital mechanics calculations in her sleep.

13

She was doing them, and she was finding answers she didn't like at all. "It's Karl," Noemi said. "He's in trouble."

# Chapter Two

Karl Muller had a tendency to brood. His moods could be dark and savage, mostly toward himself. Even when he was most depressed, though, there was one sure-fire antidote guaranteed to lift his spirits and send a thrill up his spine—just let him loose at the controls of the nearest vehicle, the higher its performance the better.

Karl's reflexes were at their peak, his hand-eye coordination were awesome, and his concentration was more acute than ever before. Beyond that, Karl knew he was lucky. He was lucky to have been born at the right time. If he'd lived in any other age throughout human history, he would have been limited to the speed and maneuverability of his own body, or that of a horse or racing camel, perhaps. He could have tried skiing, Karl supposed, but skiing had been primitive and slow back then compared to modern techniques. Trains? Gliders? Those old-time person-carrying Chinese kites? Whichever way you sliced it, thousands of Karls had lived and died without any way to satisfy their need for speed and the thrill of control.

But now there were cars, and autobahns with no speed limits. There were speedboats. There were airplanes; if things had worked out differently, Karl thought he might have become a test pilot, flying the newest and fastest and most dangerous aircraft to their limits, if not beyond. And, instead of an airplane Karl was flying the most sophisticated vehicles ever assembled, as far away from the surface of the Earth as any pilot had ever gone. Karl had been having the time of his life.

His six friends in Nathan's team were Karl's family now, along with some of the others among the one hundred thirty-five people in the crew. As with any family, there were times when he needed them and times when he couldn't bear to be on the same planet that they were. His ship was another matter. Dr. Allen may have been the chief pilot, and Karl was willing to admit that there *was* another copilot beside him, too, but that didn't matter; when he was at the controls, *Santa Maria* was *his*. When he *was* in control, in a strange way the ship felt to Karl more like a part of his own body than a separate machine. It wasn't like any other kind of relationship he'd ever felt. It was *him*.

Which made it all the more difficult to accept that things were going wrong.

The actual landing of *Santa Maria* itself hadn't

been a problem at all. The long hours of training and Karl's many trips through Dr. Allen's wringer had paid off. For *Santa Maria*'s descent to the surface Karl had been copilot behind Dr. Allen, and the Irish streetfighter Ian McShane had been handling the communications and backup boards, the three of them working as a smooth unit together with the computers and sensors to bring the ship down softly in just the right place. That hadn't been the end of the immediate job, though. There were still three cargo pods waiting in Mars-orbit to come down after them.

Karl remembered Dr. Mary Elizabeth Allen's briefing well. In addition to being *Santa Maria*'s chief pilot and the nominal leader of the expedition, she was the principal physician, chief medical officer, and the senior mission planning specialist available. Although she hadn't come right out and said it, Karl had the clear impression that the cargo pods had been her idea.

"We're talking about a big settlement here," Dr. Allen had said. "A *very* big settlement. Four hundred people. Four hundred people breathe, eat, and drink a tremendous quantity of consumable materials, and they need a fair lot of space to move around in. They need personal space, too. We're going to be living together in close quarters for a long time, and if we don't want people going bonkers we need to give them at least a little elbow room, at least enough space to get off by themselves and unwind. The logistics and resources involved in such a titanic undertaking were, shall we say, rather intimidating. No, more than that — no one thought it could actually be done, or that it was a good idea to try."

She'd called up another set of charts and figures on the briefing room monitor. "The standard wisdom was to first send a small advance team to Mars to scout locations, verify the availability of resources at the chosen settlement site, set up the initial infrastructure of shelter, air, water, food, and so forth, and then gradually build up in force from there through additional trips from Earth. Then the politicians got hold of it." Dr. Allen's smile was wan. "You're not kids anymore. I think you're learning how politics and compromise work. The result of the United Nations deliberations was our actual plan of all-at-once settlement in overwhelming force. No one was really happy with it — I know *I* wasn't — but on the other hand, it had behind it the force of international agreement."

Karl had been pleased that she'd started dealing with them as equals, not as punk youngsters. Of course, that also meant they had to begin coping with the kinds of decisions and strains the adults who'd planned the operations had had to face all along. "The only choice was to be bold," Dr. Allen was continuing. "During the early months on Mars, the settlement would have to subsist totally on supplies from Earth. With the right supplies, the settlement could use them to build up its capability to use martian resources as well, but to do that we still had to be able to live through the first months.

"You've all studied space transport design, too. You know how expensive it is to get a payload from the surface of the Earth into Earth-orbit, and from Earth to Mars. With people on board ship, the designers are limited even more. The people have to eat, drink, and breathe on the way, and the ship can't accelerate too rapidly or you get smears of goo instead of people. The bottom line is this: You have four hundred people to move to Mars, the supplies they'll consume on the way, and the supplies to sustain them for the first few months once they get there, and it turns out it can't be done. Not all together, not with the same ships carrying everything, people *and* supplies, not with the technology we have now."

Dr. Allen had smiled out at their shocked faces. "Don't worry. Like a lot of good engineering, we just had to look at the problem from a different angle. After all, the expedition doesn't need most of its supplies until it *gets* to Mars. So we send the supplies to Mars separately, by themselves. Without the need to supply air, water, and food to passengers en route, unmanned freighters could be launched months before the passenger ships on a much more leisurely and low-cost route to Mars, which means they could carry a lot more stuff, too. In fact, these freighters didn't even need to use

19

rocket fuel. They could sail."

She'd showed photographs. Vast sheets of reflective Mylar that were fractions of an inch thick by miles on a side had been assembled in Earth-orbit. Dangling from their centers were clusters of cargo pods filled with consumables, building supplies, surface rovers, personal goods, and all the thousands of items that the Mars settlers would urgently need. Under the radiation pressure or "solar wind" flowing constantly outward from the sun, the sails had been pushed in a slow drift away from the Earth's orbit and toward the orbit of Mars. Arriving at Mars in the days and weeks before the passenger ships, onboard computers had detached the cargo pods from their sails, leaving the giant sails to float even farther into the reaches of the solar system, bearing sensors and probes toward Jupiter and the outer planets. The cargo pods themselves had gone into orbit around Mars, waiting for the appearance of the human settlers whose needs they were to serve.

Now those settlers *had* appeared, of course, Karl had thought just minutes ago, settling himself back in the principal co-pilot's seat next to Dr. Allen's command chair. The passenger transports were on the ground. They had secured the area around the landing zones. With the advantage of on-site inspection, the designated sensor team had made the final selection of the best spots to set the cargo ships down. Now it was time to guide the cargo pods to join them on the surface of Mars.

"Okay, Karl," Dr. Allen had said. They were on *Santa Maria*'s flight deck, at the control boards that had let them guide the ship down from orbit not long before. "Let's do it, shall we? Watch me this time, just as we practiced."

By now the words weren't necessary, but you had to say *something*. They'd spent much of the trip from Earth in those very same seats, working on the very same tasks. "Set Flight Mode to Remote," Dr. Allen said.

"Flight Mode to Remote, Check," said Karl, following along with her on the computer flight checklist. Flight Mode was perhaps the single most critical cockpit setting to verify. It determined whether they would be flying *Santa Maria* herself, a training simulation, or one of the cargo pods. Since the flight of the original NASA Space Shuttles, the primary control systems of aircraft and spacecraft were no longer attached directly to engines, rudders, or elevons as they had been in the older days of flying. Instead, flight controls and flight displays (the monitors, readouts, gauges, and indicators that told where the ship was and reported her condition) were hooked into the ship's central computers. In a sense, the computers were really the ones doing the piloting. Using this "fly-by-wire" system, the computers had the responsibility of generating commands to the thrusters and displays for the crew on the basis of the crew's operation of their controls, measurements from sensors, and the computers'

21

own mission programming.

Using fly-by-wire, *Santa Maria*'s computers could function in several different ways. They could let the flight crew pilot *Santa Maria* itself. For testing or training, they could simulate *Santa Maria*'s behavior without actually generating maneuvering commands, allowing the flight crew to use their own controls for practice without the risk of hazard to the ship. Or for the job at hand, the computers could communicate directly with *another* spacecraft, sending it commands and receiving data back. Karl had never been a particular fan of video games, but this was one he could really get into. The illusion was complete, even without the feel of engines kicking at his back or the extra weight of high-G deceleration. He felt as though he was actually riding another ship that was really hundreds of miles away.

"We've established our communications uplink with Cargo Pod One," Ian told Dr. Allen from his position at the boards behind them. "Everything looks good. The pod's computers report all systems are go."

"Three minutes to One's de-orbit burn," Dr. Allen reported, watching her own displays. The pod's computers would probably manage its landing just fine by themselves. But there were always the emergency situations that might arise to which only a human could properly respond. In one of the most dramatic moments in the history of spaceflight, for example, during the first manned descent to the

Earth's moon, Neil Armstrong had had to take manual control of Apollo 11's *Eagle* lander just seconds from the ground to steer it away from a patch of large boulders. If the *Eagle* had flown in solely under the direction of its computer, the lander would have been destroyed and killed.

"Coming up on the mark," Karl said. "Now! Okay, we've got it!" The computer display updated rapidly. Hundreds of miles above, Cargo Pod One's rocket was firing in a precise burn, slowing its velocity and causing it to drop out of its orbit and head in a long trajectory toward the surface of Mars. "Still firing . . . cutoff!" The display told the story: a ninety-eight percent of the calculated engine burn, the exact force needed for exactly the right duration.

The pod's skin temperature began to increase, as friction with the thin Martian atmosphere began to pick up.

"There she goes," stated Ian. "Coming up on los. . . ."

"Loss of signal" was expected. Hot gases and ionized plasma from the atmosphere were now flowing around the pod, emitting so much interference of their own that it was impossible for communications signals to penetrate. This was usually the most hair-raising part of a plunge into an atmosphere — watching, waiting, and not knowing. But there was no way around it.

The seconds crept past as Karl and Dr. Allen

anxiously scanned the readouts for the first fresh news from the pod. "Straight down the track," Dr. Allen said with satisfaction as the telemetry downlink resumed.

The pod was coming in exactly on its calculated path. During the blackout period, its velocity had been slowed dramatically by the atmospheric friction. Dr. Allen's hand hovered over the controls as the timer counted toward the next mark. The cockpit screens were getting a visual feed now, too, from the television cameras in the pod. On one side an aerial view of the moving surface below, next to it the far horizon with its clear pink sky. Then suddenly the image shuddered and rocked, and a quick shadow swept over the camera view. The huge parachutes were coming out.

The digital readout of the pod's velocity wound rapidly down. Another display showed a terrain map of the surrounding section of Mars. Several lines overlaid on the map told the story of the pod's travels: its desired course as a two red lines, the actual course so far in its descent (as a green line right down the middle), and its predicted course until touchdown (a dotted continuation of the green line). A blinking crosshairs indicated the estimated point of touchdown.

Karl played with the display controls, and a new picture appeared on one of the screens. They had a quick glimpse of empty pink sky with a few wispy white clouds. Then the view zoomed rapidly into the distance as *Santa Maria*'s telescopic sight focused on the location given it by the ship's computers. "We've got the pod live," Karl said.

Seen through the telescope, the pod was still only a tiny white speck in the distance. That would change soon enough. The speck began to take on a little more of a rounded shape. From this distance, they were actually viewing the parachute, not the much smaller pod itself. Then the white shape abruptly began to tumble up out of the frame. "Parachute separation," said Dr. Allen. "And now, let's light up the engines."

A bright spot of orange-red erupted in the middle of the telescope screen. "Powering up," Dr. Allen continued.

"Look at this, mates," said Ian. "We can see ourselves!"

Karl swiveled his view to the other screen, the one showing the pictures coming from the pod itself. Ahead and below as the camera looked down, there off to one side was a small crater. The crater, yes, but just off to the south side was the shiny glint of metal in the sun — the *Santa Maria*.

"I'm going manual," Dr. Allen said. With a deft hand, she manipulated the thruster controls. The various scenes in the video pictures grew larger. The crater expanded and slipped slowly off to one side, gradually tipping over so they were looking straight down.

"The landing legs are open," Karl said. Dust and

small rocks began to rise and spin away below the pod. On the corners of the downward-looking view, the round pads of the docking feet had dropped into sight as well.

"Almost there." murmured Dr. Allen. There was the shadow of the pod itself, drawing toward the center of the screen, coming to meet the pod as it sank, slowing even more, almost hovering. Then the scene rocked, dust flew up from the feet, and the rocket flame died.

"All right!" said Karl. "Everything perfect!"

Dr. Allen permitted herself a small smile. She spoke into the small headset microphone that hung just next to her throat. "As you've already seen, Cargo Pod One has safely arrived just where we wanted it. Now we're going to go after Number Two." She turned to Karl. "Okay, flyboy, the next one is yours."

That much had been fine. It had only been moments ago, but Karl's heart had leapt with excitement as he established contact with Pod Two. The minutes dragged as they waited for the pod to come around and into position. Finally, Karl began the sequence that would lead to the same smooth succession of computer-driven steps. He felt completely in control. There hadn't been another place in the universe he would rather have been.

Until the trouble started.

Pod Two's engine had started its burn okay. It hadn't been quite as clean as One's, perhaps, but it was still well within the design tolerance. The engine just hadn't cut off on schedule, that was all.

Karl had been watching all the readouts, not missing the quiver of a single meter, so he'd begun to react in a fraction of a second when the engine missed its shutdown mark. There was a manual shutdown that would override the pod's on-board computer. Karl had hit it immediately. The pod hadn't listened. The rocket kept firing. He reached to cut out the pod's computer entirely.

Wait a second—the pod *had* listened. Its computer was reporting that the message had been received. In fact, the pod's computer was still trying to shut down the engine itself.

Time seemed to stretch for Karl like taffy. Probably only a second or two had actually elapsed, but every second was sending the pod farther off its course. If it didn't follow precisely the right trajectory, the best that could happen was that the pod would land far from its correct landing spot. Even worse, the pod could tumble or burn up when it entered the atmosphere, and one-third of the colony's supplies would be lost in a red-hot fireball!

# Chapter Three

*What was wrong?* Karl asked himself frantically. Next to him, Dr. Allen was tapping furiously at her own computer.

Karl seized the thruster controls. The pod's engine nozzle was mounted on gimbals, like the main engines on the Space Shuttle. It could be swiveled from side to side to steer the engine's force. With a sharp twist to the right and then a matching one back to the left, Karl jerked the control around.

"What are you doing?" Dr. Allen snapped. "You're going to—"

The computers were reporting that the pod's engine had finally shut down. The pod's computer had continued to send the turn-off signal. Now, for some reason, the engine had listened.

"I thought the main fuel valve might have been stuck," Karl explained, his face white. "If I'd been standing next to it I would have kicked it or hit it with a wrench. Since I wasn't, I thought shaking the pod might be the next best thing."

"Good thinking, boyo," Ian said.

"It seems to have worked," Dr. Allen said slowly. "I think you were right."

"But it took me so long," Karl said mournfully. He had a horrible sensation in his stomach. The pod was probably still doomed. His abrupt maneuver might have made things even worse, sending it even farther off course. If he'd reacted faster, it still might have been possible to correct the pod's course and bring it in on target.

The pod was hitting the atmosphere, and contact was cut off. *Santa Maria*'s computers were busily trying to calculate the pod's fate. The terrain map came up, a series of shaded ellipses like a tilted bull's-eye covering the surface to the northeast of the base's position. That was the estimated impact zone. Somewhere in that shaded area the pod would be coming down. Would it be as a flaming meteorite or would there still be a chance of getting it under control?

Noemi had been right. Karl was definitely in trouble. Nathan's entire team was now glued to the monitor, and other people were drifting up to join them. "What do you think, Noemi?" Nathan asked.

She was chewing the side of her lip. "It doesn't look good," she admitted. "That pod is going to come in like a big rock." She tilted her head to one side and shrugged in a quick graceful move. A brief

29

glimpse of the old Noemi glamour girl they'd known on Earth.

"Oh, no!" Gen said suddenly, clapping one hand over his forehead. "Not Pod Two!"

"Not Pod Anything," Lanie said. "If that thing goes down we're all going to get pretty thin. That's a third of our food and seeds for the greenhouse." She'd pulled up Pod Two's cargo manifest from the computer and was quickly scanning it. "We may have to breathe in shifts, too."

"There it is!" Karl said. The pod's signals had just begun to break through the interference from its fiery entry into the atmosphere. The mere fact that they were hearing from it again meant that the pod hadn't burned up. *Santa Maria*'s computers talked rapidly back and forth with the pod, and the estimated landing zone graphic on the map shrunk as the information on the pod's altitude, speed, and heading were processed to figure out its new trajectory. It hadn't burned up. On the other hand, it was hundreds of miles off course and was coming down way too fast.

"Don't release the parachute," warned Dr. Allen. At its present velocity, the parachute would be ripped to shreds.

"I'm going to fire the engine," Karl said, his teeth clenched, as he activated the controls. A quick spurt, that's all it needed, she hoped.

The faulty valve held, the engine fired, and the

pod's velocity dropped. On the map, the landing zone slid a bit closer to their own position. "Watch your fuel consumption," Dr. Allen reminded.

"That should be enough," said Karl. He hit the shutoff command and held his breath.

This time, the engine had throttled down precisely as planned. The parachute let loose, the pod rocked and shuddered, but the chute stayed intact. "You don't have enough fuel left for a soft landing," said Dr. Allen.

It was true. The pod would still crash-land.

"Look at the map," Karl said. "Look where it's coming down now."

*Santa Maria*'s landing site was in the same corner of the Mars as some of the planet's most interesting terrain. Eight hundred miles northeast of *Santa Maria*'s position, the ground began to rise. They had set down southwest of the titanic Olympus Mons, the most massive known volcano in the whole solar system. Everest, the largest mountain on Earth, rises 5.5 miles above sea level, but Everest would barely be a foothill for Olympus Mons, a monster 17 miles high and 370 miles wide. Olympus Mons was so tall it stuck out above the top of the Martian atmosphere!

As if that wasn't enough, a thousand miles east of the landing site was the Tharsis bulge. In a thousand-mile line running from southwest to northeast, the crust of Mars was uplifted to a height of 5.5 miles above the terrain of Mars. On top of that were three other extinct volcanoes. Although each of the

Tharsis volcanoes was only six miles high, this was measured from the base of an already gigantic bulge. As a result, the Tharsis summits were nearly as high as the top of Olympus Mons.

The mother ships and the cargo pods had been orbiting the planet in a track almost directly above its equator and traveling from east to west. Because of the pod's malfunction it was coming down too soon. Its landing zone would now lie in the midst of the Tharsis bulge, almost at the base of the Pavonis Mons, the middle of the three Tharsis volcanoes. The pod's fuel tanks had been drained low by Karl's extra braking maneuver and would run dry with the pod still miles above the altitude at *Santa Maria*'s base. The ground where the pod was coming down wasn't at *Santa Maria*'s altitude, however — ground level at that point on the Tharsis bulge where the pod would land was still over five miles higher than *Santa Maria*. The ground should come up under the pod just around the same time its fuel gave out.

Dr. Allen reviewed the situation carefully as Karl prepared to jettison the parachute. "I think we can make it," she said cautiously.

"Stay loose, boyo," said Ian.

The parachute drifted up and away, and again Karl fired up the engine. The ground came closer, the fuel gauge dropped, dust flew. Karl could almost feel it when the engine coughed and died, its fuel exhausted. The pod bounced and juggled on its landing struts, rocked, and then settled to a rest intact.

"I'm glad that was you and not me," Ian said.

"That was very professionally done," added Dr. Allen.

"That's it for me," Karl mumbled in a dejected voice. "I really blew it." He realized his hands were still locked around the controls in a grip so strong that his fingers were white. Karl forced himself to let go. When he did so, his hands began to shake.

"It's time to bring in the third pod," Dr. Allen told him.

"You do it. Or Ian. I just . . . I just—" He would screw up the third one even worse than the second, Karl just knew it.

"No," directed Dr. Allen. "Stay right where you are. You are going to control that third pod, and you are going to do it now. That's an order."

"Yes, ma'am," Karl said reluctantly. "But I don't—"

"That's enough," Dr. Allen told him. "Just concentrate and you'll be fine."

That was easy for *her* to say. Karl established communications with Pod Three, a feeling of dread hovering over him. The settlement *could* survive with the supplies from two of the three pods—barely, if nothing went wrong, but food and water and materials and everything else would be very tight. If Karl lost the third pod, too, though, they would all probably be doomed.

"It's coming up on the ignition mark," Dr. Allen warned him. He didn't trust himself to speak, so he just gave a small quick nod, not taking his eyes from the readouts for an instant. The pod's engine lit exactly on schedule and throttled up, and again the seconds crept agonizingly by.

"Three seconds to cutoff. Two . . . One . . . Zero."

The meters showing thrust and propellant flow fell back. Engine temperature dropped. It had worked! They had gotten past the hurdle that had tripped Karl with the previous pod.

But he couldn't relax, not yet. The most important part of his task still stretched ahead. Pod Three entered its blackout period. Karl chewed his lip, running through all the emergency procedures in his mind, trying to remember every last scrap of his lengthy and demanding training. When the pod reestablished contact, right down the center of its desired trajectory, it was almost anticlimactic.

Karl didn't complain.

The parachute popped and slowed the craft as scheduled, and then the engine reignited on cue. Karl took direct control and brought it smoothly down a short distance away from Pod One. "You see?" Dr. Allen commented. "That was fine."

Karl slumped in his seat and closed his eyes. He was soaked with sweat. He was so relieved he could hardly speak. "If I hadn't done that just now I'd never have been able to touch a flight panel again," he said weakly.

"I know," said Dr. Allen.

# Chapter Four

The complicated process of setting up the settlement began to get into gear. The computer jockeys and the executive planning group had been up all night analyzing the resource situation and setting up new schedules and new priorities for the work ahead of them. The communications channels back to Earth had been busy, too, as the larger computers and teams of specialists on Earth provided what additional thoughts and help they could. Ultimately, the final decisions and final responsibility for the Mars base rested with the Mars settlers themselves. When signals traveling at the speed of light took fifteen minutes just to make the one-way trip from Mars to Earth, there was no other system that made sense.

Nathan stood outside the airlock in his full pressure suit watching the sun come up as the morning sky turned pink instead of blue. The sun looked smaller than on Earth. During the long trip, they had watched the sun shrink as they moved away from it. They had watched the Earth shrink, too. When you were standing on the Earth you weren't even conscious you were on the surface of a planet—the ground seemed flat, and the horizon was so far away. By the time you got into orbit around Earth, there was no denying it. The blue and green and white ball dominating the heavens, hanging there without any support at all, was certainly a planet. And not just *any* planet, either, but *home*. Heading toward Mars had been exciting, but watching the giant ball of Earth dwindle to the size of a small coin and then a blue-green-tinged sparkle had been hard. Now, the Earth was just another light in the sky.

Nathan watched as the other team members started assembling on the Mars's surface. They were all wearing their pressure suits. Mars *did* have an atmosphere of sorts, but it wasn't breathable. The Earth's atmosphere was mostly made up of nitrogen and oxygen, with smaller amounts of things like water vapor and carbon dioxide, but the atmosphere surrounding them now was almost totally carbon dioxide. There was some water vapor—Nathan could see some wisps of ground fog still clinging to the hollows behind rocks and lurking in the shadows of gullies—but very little oxygen. Far too little oxygen for a person to survive on. The Martian atmosphere was also much thinner than Earth's. At the expedition's landing site, the pressure was only one one-hundredth of the pressure at sea level on Earth.

Okay, so they couldn't breathe on the surface of Mars, and they couldn't survive the low pressures without some kind of protective suit. Unfortunately, their problems didn't end there. A thinner atmosphere meant more than just not being able to breathe. The Earth's thick atmosphere trapped heat from the sun. The major difference between the comfortable surface of the Earth and the frozen and hostile surface of Earth's moon, in fact, was the effect of the Earth's blanket of air. Mars's atmosphere was far too slight to retain much heat at all. The typical temperatures at the base would be about sixty-five degrees Fahrenheit below zero. If they had to travel to the poles, though, they'd be facing a frozen bed of carbon dioxide ice as much as two hundred degrees below zero. It might not be a total loss. If they were lucky, they might be able to catch a few decent rays now and then during summer, when it might even warm up to a balmy eighty-five degrees *above* zero. At least that's what they'd been told. Nathan wasn't about to wait up for it.

The humans would also have to keep a close watch on their detectors for radiation and ultraviolet rays. Earth's atmosphere was pretty good at screening the sun's harmful particles and radiation from its surface. Again, Mars's atmosphere would let almost all of this dangerous stuff through. They'd probably be okay most of the time, at the sun's normal level of radiation, since the space suits and the ships would shield them to a certain extent. Even though they were past the peak of the sun's eleven-year sunspot cycle, however, it would still be necessary to be alert. The sun could emit a flare at any time. During a typical solar flare, the sun's output of radiation could increase by a factor of ten within a matter of hours. They had all felt its power to disrupt communication months ago on *Icarus*.

Once they opened up the cargo pods and started unloading their supplies and gear, they'd at least get a bit of a break as far as their clothing went. The hard space suits they'd used on the trip and on the descent, and were still wearing now, in fact, were pretty much the same kind of equipment first used in the early 1960's by the first astronauts. But unlike those older suits, which could only withstand fairly low pressures, the ones they were wearing now could be pressurized to the relatively high pressures inside the ship. If they were still using the old suits, they'd have had to breathe pure oxygen for hours every time they wanted to go outside or risk a painful or debilitating attack of the "bends." Even so, their hard-suits were big and bulky and not particularly comfortable. Their gloves, in particular, didn't give any sensation about what they might be touching and made fine control difficult. It was hard to work in them. Inside the cargo pods, though, were the new suits that had been designed for them to use on the Martian surface. Getting to the new suits was one of the first jobs for Nathan's team.

"Yo, fearless leader!" a voice crackled in Nathan's helmet headset. Lanie had been up part of the night running simulations and computer projections and had to be dead tired, but was she going to miss this? No way. At least that's what she'd told Nathan in no uncertain terms when he suggested she sit this one out and grab some sleep. "Let's get it in gear!"

A mixed chorus of "Yeah"s and "Let's do it!"s agreed with her.

"You've got it, gang," said Nathan, starting to turn away from the sunrise screen. Then something in the sky caught his attention—a bluish star hanging not far above the sun. It wasn't a star. It was the Earth.

Nathan felt a gloved hand on his shoulder. "Quite a sight, my friend, is it not?" said Sergei. "Can you see . . ."

"What?" Nathan said. Sergei had the sharpest eyesight of anyone on the team. Nathan glanced at him. Behind the gold radiation-screening visor covering the faceplate of his helmet, Sergei was squinting intently at the rising Earth.

"I see a faint brown dot just next to the blue one, next to the Earth," Sergei said finally. "It is dim, but it is quite apparent. The Moon."

"Stop sightseeing and get this act on the road," muttered Lanie. Their radios were all turned to the same frequency. They could communicate among themselves without broadcasting to everybody in the vicinity, but it made it difficult to have any kind of private talk. Each work team had its own frequency channel, and another special channel was reserved at all times for emergency and general warning information, but with all the people in the expedition the available channels would fill up quickly as the work day got underway.

Nathan's team was not the first group up and

39

about, either. As Nathan turned and led them north, the could see two teams out ahead of them, and another was making its way out of *Santa Maria*'s airlock behind them. "Move slowly until you get your bearings," Nathan warned. The gravity took some getting used to.

"This is odd," agreed Gen.

"It's kind of like wearing high heels," said Noemi. "I mean, it's not *really* like high heels, but you sort of have to balance yourself just right if you don't want to trip and fall over."

As if she'd been listening to her, Tara White suddenly windmilled her arms and *did* fall over, narrowly missing Lisette in front of her. Karl helped her up.

"Try this," suggested Karl. Karl, the best athlete of the team, did everything physical with his own natural grace. It was no surprise that he'd be the one to figure this out. He moved out in front. Karl was, well . . . *skipping*, sort of, with his right leg out in front and his left in back, keeping his feet fairly low to the ground and moving slowly.

It *did* work better than the good old one-foot-in-front-of-the-other. "Thanks. How did you think this up?" Tara asked Karl.

"It was not my idea," Karl admitted. "The original astronauts on the Moon did much the same thing, if you remember the films."

"Didn't catch them, but maybe . . . hey—"

Karl just turned and walked away.

"What's with the boy wonder?" Tara asked Lisette. "He probably still kicking himself over Cargo Pod

40

Two. You know how he gets when he finds out he's not perfect."

"He'll work it out, I guess."

Karl slowed to pick his way carefully through a jumble of rocks. With the sun now fully risen, the powerful red-orange color of the dirt and rocks had leapt out at them with startling clarity. All those iron oxides made it look like some maniac painter had been set loose on the set design for some space epic.

On his left, the ground rose slightly to end in an abrupt line against the sky less than two hundred feet away. That line was the rim of the nearest crater. The crater was small, only eight hundred feet or so in diameter, but it was the reason they'd selected this spot to land. Craters were not rare on Mars; far from it, in fact. Most of the southern hemisphere was covered with them.

The Martian craters were caused by the same things that had caused the craters on the Earth's moon — big pieces of rock slamming into the surface. The shock wave as an asteroid or meteorite hit and vaporized would have blown open the crater itself. Immediately after the shock wave there would have been a low-pressure wave that would suck debris out of the crater and throw it across the surrounding landscape. This "ejecta blanket" was what Karl and the others were making their way across now.

"Rocks," said Noemi. "More rocks. Somebody should clean this place up."

"Are you volunteering?" said Gen.

Up ahead, a squat cone shape rose to a slightly

squared-off point. Perhaps one hundred yards behind it was a second one—the cargo pods. Pod Three was the closer of the two. They looked like a cross between a cartoon stereotype of a space nose cone with tripod landing legs, only short and fat. Their wide bottoms gave them an ungainly look. All that wide space, though, was there to hold cargo. Once it was empty, it would help to hold *them*.

Pod Three's loading ramp had already been lowered out of the bottom section of its hull by the first team to arrive. As Nathan's team came up to the base of the ramp, lights around the cargo door came on as well. Just inside the door they were confronted by a wall of solid boxes and containers of equipment and supplies.

The whole cargo manifest was on computer, showing where each container was and what was inside of it. In the replanning sessions last night, they had revised the unloading order, but the new one was on line, too. Everyone set to work.

The sun traveled across the sky with deceptive familiarity, just about as fast as it had done on Earth. One day on Mars, in fact, was only about forty minutes longer than a day on Earth. The planners had toyed with the idea of adding the extra time as "leap minutes" after midnight, but had finally decided to stretch out each second and minute in a slow, gradual process that everyone had adjusted to while they were still on board ship on the way to Mars. However, everything seemed to have worked out. When their watches said it was twelve noon and time for a brief break, the sun was just overhead and they felt like they'd put in a normal morning of hard work.

"Ow!" said Noemi. "I think my fingers are bleeding. These gloves are awful! I can't feel a thing through them."

"Nobody said this place would be a resort," Lanie said, squirming to find a convenient and comfortable way to sit down in the bulky suit. They had all gathered on the cargo ramp.

"Don't be babies," said Gen. "This place is cool. Ten thousand people would trade places with you in an instant. Especially if they like orange juice." He turned his head and took a pull from the juice tube in his helmet.

"I wish I could at least look forward to a long hot bath when we get back to the ship," Noemi said wistfully.

She was greeted by a chorus of groans. Not one of them would have minded such a luxury, either. Unfortunately hot baths were a long way in their future.

"You could take a bath in your suit," suggested Nathan. It might have been far below freezing outside, but inside his suit it was comfortable, or even a bit toasty from the heat he'd worked up shifting and dragging. The problem was really one of not getting too hot! Without a special cooling system, the insulating effect of the suit combined with the slow rate of heat loss to the environment would have gradually roasted him. Instead, underneath the suit, Nathan was wearing a leotardlike garment with cooling tubes woven through it. Water circulating through the tubes and out to the radiator fins on his backpack let the temperature inside the suit remain comfortable.

"Enough of this laziness," said Karl, sucking down the last sips of his high protein shake. "It is time to get into some serious work." He pushed himself smoothly to his feet.

"Workers of the world, unite," muttered Sergei. "Very well. If you must play hot rod in that thing, I suppose someone responsible should look out for you." He climbed to his feet as well.

The "thing" Sergei had referred to was sitting at the lower end of the cargo ramp. It had been the first piece of equipment unloaded from the pod, and at least they hadn't had to lift *it*. Once they had opened up its storage "garage," had unfastened it from its restraints, and had powered it up, the Mars rover had driven itself out on its own. It wasn't a high-performance speed machine, but the rover and its siblings in Pod One and the lost Pod Two were as close as he was going to get on Mars, so Karl had gotten his dibs in early.

Not that anyone seriously quarreled with him, Nathan thought, watching Karl ease himself back into the driver's seat. Other people would drive the vehicles, too, since it would be foolhardy to have only one qualified motorist per machine, but there was no doubt that Karl's talent for handling anything that moved was superb. If they'd had a chariot around, or a dogsled, Nathan was sure that Karl would be the one in charge of them as well.

The rover was basically a dune buggy, although

dune buggies on Earth did not usually sport a large parabolic antenna, attachments for a bulldozer blade and a forklift, and a trailer hitch. Earth-bound dune buggies also had more comfortable seats, too. Of course, this vehicle was a workhorse, not a party animal.

Dune buggies on Earth weren't built in modules, either. This one, though, was designed for maximum flexibility. Additional cartlike sections could be attached in back, each one able to pivot at the point of attachment. If you added enough sections, the rover would look more like a caterpillar than a normal vehicle. Some of the modules were unpowered trailers, but some had their own propulsion motors so that with the right configuration, the vehicle could haul around quite a lot of stuff.

Like virtually all of their equipment, the rovers ran on electric power rather than fuel. At the moment, that power was being provided by batteries that would be recharged from the ship at night. A bit later on, when the settlement was able to produce chemical supplies from mining or refining, the batteries would be replaced by more powerful fuel cells generating electricity from the reaction between oxygen and hydrogen.

The largest containers of supplies were packed on the lowest level of the cargo pod. Someone had been doing his job right, Nathan thought as they got back to work. Rather than making them manhandle these containers out of the ship and onto trailers, or having to use the rover's forklift module on every last item, the containers had been shipped already attached to their trailers. They needed to ship the trailers, too, after all, so why not put them where they'd immediately be useful? As it was, they could back the rover up the ramp into the hold right up to a trailer, hitch it on, and then drive it carefully down the ramp and off to wherever it was going.

Initially, some of the stuff was going directly to the *Santa Maria* and some was being carefully arranged and stacked between the pod and the edge of the crater, but some equipment was being unpacked right next to the pod. Several of the first containers they'd pulled out had immediately been taken over by another work team. Inside were sheet after sheet of strong but lightweight solar cells. The other team was already setting them up. They had fenced off a baseball diamond-size patch of reasonably flat ground between the pods and the *Santa Maria* and a bit farther out from the crater. It would not take long before that entire field would be covered by solar panels generating the kilowatts of electricity the settlement would initially need.

When you got right down to it, Nathan reflected, lifting and dragging and unpacking was not very stimulating work. If you were going to be a pioneer, though, there were things you had to do to stay alive. One of his mother's ancestors had been a homesteader in Revolutionary War-era Kentucky, and several generations later another ancestor had moved out to scratch a living from the Great Plains. Their days would have been filled with chopping wood, plowing fields, pumping water, and the thousand other physical chores you had to do because there was no one else to do them. In a way, though, Nathan thought his ancestors' stimulation and satisfaction would have come from just being there, from matching themselves against a hostile environment and holding their own, from breaking new ground for themselves and their families.

At least on Mars they didn't have to worry about wars or desperadoes or wild animals. Just physics and chemistry and resource levels and consumption rates. And, of course, whatever curves the universe chose to throw at them. It was nice that the universe seemed to be giving them a break today. Nothing dropped and broke, everything mechanical functioned smoothly the way its specifications demanded, no one had trouble with their suits, and so by the time the sun was heading for the western horizon, each team had exceeded their work targets for the day.

Noemi and Gen hitched a ride on the rover with Karl as he drove slowly toward the *Santa Maria*. On this last trip of the day, the rover was pulling a small train of two- and four-wheeled trailers piled with an assortment of large boxes and wrapped parcels. That low gravity was coming in handy for all this moving, that was for sure, Nathan thought, looking up at the piles of cargo as he trudged along behind the cart.

"Karl, slow down a moment," he heard Sergei say over the radio. Sergei was on the other side of the trailers. He and Nathan were watching to make certain nothing came loose, and Lanie was similarly bringing up the rear. "I would like to check one of the tie-downs."

"Just a moment," said Karl. "I cannot just jam on the brakes, not with these many trailers." Still, he brought the caravan to a reasonably speedy but smooth halt.

"Yes," Sergei said. "This one was coming loose. Noemi is right, these gloves are not designed well. There—it is secured."

Nathan had the hand-held computer containing the manifest of the contents of the pod and their unloading order that had been downloaded from the ship's computer. By scanning the bar codes imprinted on the labels of the various containers into his portable computer's reader, he had been able to stay on top of and coordinate their work. "Do you know what's in this crate you were tying down?" he asked Sergei.

"I am sure you are about to tell me," Sergei said dryly. The rover ground into motion again and they began trudging along with it.

"Some of the new suits, that's what."

"I am in line first,—" responded Sergei promptly.

"I'll fight you for it!" Noemi broke in.

"You don't fool me, my savage friend," Sergei told her. "But I am a gentleman, so I will give you my place. Manners are the oil that lubricates civilization."

"Just don't go getting that grease all over your clothes, that's all *I* can say," inserted Lanie.

48

*Manners,* thought Nathan. Sergei had gone through some interesting changes since Nathan had first met him. Sergei liked girls, and of course there was nothing necessarily wrong with that, but he'd been a lot better at acquiring girlfriends than at figuring out what to do with them. Now, though, he was serious about getting more responsible. His friend Ludmilla from back in Leningrad was on *Niña.* She had always thought their relationship was much heavier than Sergei did, but he'd never be willing to face her and get things straight. On the voyage out from Earth, Nathan had always been able to tell when one of Ludmilla's messages had arrived. Sergei would turn an unappetizing shade of light green and would talk about how he was too young and too appealing to make a commitment to one girl. After some of the things they'd gone through, however, Sergei had sworn those days were behind him. He was a new man.

They soon arrived back at *Santa Maria.* A line of figures in space suits stretched from each of the two personnel airlocks, waiting for their turn to enter. The rover from Pod Three was already parked over on one side, its recharger cable looping along the ground to one of the umbilical sockets in the side of the ship. "You are all welcome to get in the queue," said Karl, "but there is another option. Are you all too exhausted, or does anyone wish to help with the garage?"

"What garage?" said Noemi. "I don't see a garage."

"That is just the point," Karl said. "It is still on one

of these trailers. It must be set up."

"I'm game," said Nathan. "I think I've got the assembly instructions in this computer. Yes, here they are. They say it's a four-person job. Check your tanks"

Seeing that they had plenty of air, everyone decided to wait around and pitch in if necessary. Then they would all make their grand entrance back into the ship together. Nathan uncoupled the last several trailers from the first one, leaving the rover pulling only the parts of the collapsed garage. To the right of the closer of the small airlocks, with the capacity of handling two people at one time, was a larger airlock door. As they drove up, another team had just finished moving a big container into the airlock and squeezing themselves in after it; they dogged the door down behind them and started the airlock cycle.

Karl drove the rover up toward the door and made a three-point turn, ending with the rover pointing away from the ship and the back end of the trailer facing the door. About twenty feet of space separated the trailer from the hull of the ship.

Atop the two-wheeled trailer was a rectangular parcel about six feet wide and four feet long wrapped in a plastic covering with pull tabs on the sides. "First we unhitch the trailer, tip it over, and undo the straps," Nathan said, reading instructions off the small computer screen. In a few moments, this was accomplished, and the mysterious parcel was sitting by itself on the ground. The wrapping came free easily when they pulled on the convenient tabs.

"It's in four pieces," said Lanie. "Is that right?"

"Looks like four to me," Nathan agreed. There were indeed four identical assemblies stacked on top of each other. Each one had a carefully folded pile of thin but tough see-through plastic, some light metal rods, and two hard plates the full six-by-four size. Nathan and Sergei took hold of each side of the top assembly and walked it over next to the ship. "Like a tent, yes?" said Sergei.

It was indeed rather like a tent. When fitted together, the metal rods made a box framework twelve feet wide and four deep, with a ten-foot ceiling. The transparent plastic went up the side walls and across the top, and the two plates fitted together smoothly to form the floor. Before raising the ceiling up, though, the group placed the other four sections in their own places stretching away from the first. The edges of each segment of plastic zipped up against the next, and an overlapping flap sealed tightly across the zippers. Each end had its own special attachment: the far one could be zipped open entirely to serve as the garage door. The side closest to the ship, though, was different. Concealed behind a strip of hull metal, which they now removed, was another zipper attachment that went all around the larger airlock. Another piece of the strong plastic served to bridge the space between the hull and the edge of the garage tent.

Working together, the team lifted the plastic and finished fastening together the side supports. Then they all stood back to admire their handiwork. A transparent box now protruded from *Santa Maria*'s hull, complete with a short access ramp at the far end. Karl got back onto the rover and carefully drove it in through the open door flap. "This is good!" said Karl, looking around him. "Now at least something is settled in its new home. It is secure from dust storms, it is—"

"We're not going to pressurize the garage now, are we?" interrupted Noemi.

"I would think it would be best to leave that for special occasions," Karl said. "Such as if we have to work on the rover and cannot do it with gloves on."

"Then I for one think it's time to get inside and get these suits off," said Noemi.

No one could quarrel with that. The big airlock at the back of the garage was for use when large things needed to be brought in and out of the ship, as they had seen earlier, but for now they could use it in another way. It would fit all seven of them at once. They trooped in and cycled the door shut behind them.

On the bulkhead above the airlock controls, a sign lit up saying "Remember—Vacuum First!"

"I nearly forgot!" Noemi said. "I never thought I'd want to skip cleaning myself off, but I guess there is always a first time."

"No way around it," said Nathan. "Who's first?"

Three vacuum-cleaner hoses were mounted on the walls, and they took turns using them on each other and on the equipment they had brought in with them. The orange surface dust had gotten all over them and everything else in the course of the day. It was not just a problem of cleanliness, though. The Martian dust would cause severe lung damage if they were to breathe it, so the dust had to stay outside.

Finally, all traces of the dust had been mopped up, and at last they could reenter the ship. Air hissed into the airlock, the pressure in the airlock reached the same level as inside the ship, and the inner door opened for them. As they trooped through, Sergei said brightly, "Who wants to raid the hub with me?"

His only answer was a chorus of groans and a nasty noise or two. "All I want to do is sleep for a week," said Noemi, pulling off her helmet and stowing it in her assigned wall rack. "Then maybe I'll be ready for a vacation. Nothing is going to stop me between here and my bunk — not even food."

That went for him, too, thought Nathan. Unfortunately a vacation wasn't in the cards. "Get a good night's sleep, then," he told them. "Tomorrow's a big day."

"Yes?" said Noemi. "What do we do then?"

"We get up tomorrow and do this all again."

# Chapter Five

That was the way it went. Up before dawn, lift and carry and drag all day, or until their bodies gave out, struggle back to the ship, and collapse in exhaustion. It was not romantic. It was not, to put it plainly, what any of them had thought of as adventure. Except, of course, for the place where they happened to be doing it. And the consequences if they gave in to boredom or gave in to exhaustion or just plain gave up. Personal survival was a strong motivator.

And, too, by the end of the first week they were clearly making big progress. The pods were pretty much unloaded. Their contents had been sorted out and were beginning to be put to use. The solar power grid was operational. The construction work of installing partitions, life support systems, and amenities into the former cargo pods to convert them into living space was underway. Along with these tasks, the *really* big work was getting into gear as well.

To no one's surprise, Karl had firmly established his reputation as the best rover driver on Mars. Not that the task had been all that demanding, Karl didn't hesitate to point out himself. His bad mood over the mishap with Pod Two notwithstanding, or perhaps even because of it, Karl was eager for a new challenge, one that would push him beyond the demands of a truck-and-forklift operator in a space suit. With all the jobs in front of them that needed to be done, however, Karl's opportunity soon came up.

"We're here," said Nathan, pointing to their neighborhood crater on the high-resolution image displayed on the big monitor. The expedition had left a variety of stuff in orbit around the planet, including two satellites equipped for assisting communications on the ground and back and forth to Earth. These satellites also had a full complement of ground-scanning sensors. Their cameras, in fact, could resolve details as small as six inches across on the surface of Mars. The satellite image to which Nathan was referring was not showing that level of magnification, since the area he wanted to talk about was miles across. There was no trouble picking out their neighborhood crater, though, or even the white-and-black body of *Santa Maria* and the two pods against the bright orange of the surrounding surface. The image had been taken midway through the previous afternoon, when the slanting shadows of the spacecraft, the crater walls, and assorted boulders and hills helped to give a three-dimensional relief to the scene.

The crater and their base were off in the lower left-hand corner of the image. Nathan pointed up and to the right. An irregular blotch of silvery orange broke up the more homogeneous orange of the surrounding hills. "This is where *Santa Maria*'s parachute came down," Nathan continued. "It's about six miles out, as the crow flies, you might say."

Karl was leaning over, intent on the display, his arms on his knees. "We do not have a crow. Unless someone has been unpacking supplies I don't know about? But of course not. So how far is the real route?"

Nathan fingered his keyboard. Too bad their computers didn't have full-scale voice control yet. With luck they'd get an upgrade in one of their resupply shipments from Earth. The route-planning display showed a green line on the map zigzagging back and forth in jerky straight-line segments as it stretched from the base to the location of the parachute. "Closer to eight miles, then, actual walking distance," Nathan said, reading off the data from the summary window that had popped up along with the path line.

"Could it be done in a day, do you think?" Alice asked. The three of them were huddled together in one corner of the commons. Around them, the room was filled with other small groups of people discussing their plans for the next day in low voices.

"This leg would be no problem, I think," stated Karl, "but I believe Nathan is not yet finished."

"You're not getting to know me or anything, now, are you, Karl?" Nathan said with a chuckle. "You're right, of course." He manipulated the controls and two other shiny ground patches sprang into highlight in roughly the same area as the parachute he'd already pointed out. "Both pods had chutes, too. That's where *they* are. Since all three ships came down in the same trajectory and had pretty much the same sequencing, the chutes released at the same spot and drifted down more or less alike. Which means . . ." he paused as more green lines traced themselves out, linking *Santa Maria*'s chute and the two others before looping back toward the base—which means it's only twenty, twenty-one miles round trip to take in all three."

"Maximum design speed of the rover is forty miles per hour," said Karl. "At least that's what it says in the manual."

"Which means you could push it to forty-five, *fifty* easily," Alice commented.

"Whatever you people think, I am not a hot-rod driver," Karl told him. "I have not yet had the vehicle up to anywhere near twenty. We only have two of them. I don't want one damaged because of some foolish stunt."

"Calm down," said Alice. "Calm down. It was only a joke. We all know how responsible you are."

"Very well," said Karl. "Even if we allow a good margin of safety and plan on a low speed, we should be able to do this safely in one day. When do we start?"

"At dawn, tomorrow morning."

Driving right at dawn or sunset was one of the most dangerous times, since pitfalls could lurk in the shadows that were still long and deep. With the rover's high power headlights pointed ahead of them, and the on-board computer tracking their progress against the projected route on the orbital imaging maps, they should be okay. Alice turned to gaze past the bouncing trailers at the three towers of pods and *Santa Maria* retreating behind them as they moved away to the north, hit their first mark, and turned off to the northeast. "This is the farthest any of us has been from the base," said Alice. "Is this adventure?"

"It will do for now," said Karl. One of his intent smiles was fixed on his face behind the gold of his faceplate.

"So it will," Alice said, "so it will. And there is actual danger."

There was indeed, Nathan reflected. If anything went wrong with the vehicle, they would have to walk back. Theoretically, the suits would be good for seventy-two hours. If they had to walk they'd be betting their lives on that performance. They'd probably be outside in the night, too, which would

58

pose its own problems.

Karl had a good eye and good judgment, which were at least as important as motor skill for the task of traversing the Martian terrain. Choosing the best path through a field of rocks ranging in size from the litter of pebbles and gravel to boulders taller than the rover was a skill that spelled the difference between feeling their way gingerly along, constantly stopping, and making smooth progress.

The expedition had landed in the region of Mangala Vallis, just on the Martian equator. "Mangala" was the Sanskrit word for Mars, and "Vallis" was just "Valley," so it was really sort of a generic name when you tried to tease it apart. From orbit, Mangala Vallis was a channel that looked as though it had been carved out by flowing water. There was no surface water now, of course, but the conclusion that at some time in the remote past there had been was inescapable. Or was it? One of the tasks of the expedition would be to try to settle the question one way or another.

Mangala Vallis was at the boundary between the rough terrain, full of craters and obstacles, that covered the southern hemisphere, and the much smoother volcanic plains of the north. "Smoother," though, didn't necessarily mean "smooth." If the three of them hadn't been wearing seat belts, Nathan was sure there were times when he would have been catapulted completely out of the side of the rover.

59

"Yow!" said Nathan as Karl ran the right-side wheels over the side of a small boulder. "Don't do that!"

"A backseat driver, are you then?" Karl commented.

"I *am* in the backseat," said Alice, "and it is all I can do to stay there, I will have you know."

"Would you rather I be driving over more regular terrain? Very well, then." Karl eased the wheel over and angled the vehicle a bit to the left, up a low rise which they soon topped. "And so," said Karl.

The ground on the other side was much flatter and significantly more even as well. The larger rocks were fewer and further apart. They would have no trouble steering around them.

"Runoff channels," mused Nathan. "That could have been an old streambed we were driving in. All those big rocks could have been swept downstream and left in the mud."

"Just as long as it doesn't happen again *while* we're driving in it," said Alice.

The ship was out of sight. Their radios operated primarily on line-of-sight transmissions, since Mars lacked the Earth's convenient ionosphere to bounce communications around the curve of the planet. One of the communications satellites was in position as a relay station, though, so they were still able to check in with the ship as necessary.

"What's that?" said Alice, shielding her eyes. "Up ahead and a little bit to the left?" Something was

60

shining in the sunlight. "Is that the first chute?"

Karl checked his instruments. They had come the right distance, and in the right direction. "I believe it is," he agreed.

*Santa Maria*'s parachute was draped across the dirt and rocks, partly folded under itself, with some of the shroud lines trailing across the open ground toward them as they approached. It looked to Nathan like a football-field-size bedsheet spread out to dry, or perhaps a circus tent with its poles and rigging kicked out from under it. "Please stop for a moment," Alice asked.

Karl eased off the motor and carefully applied the brakes. "Have you noticed something wrong?" he said.

"No," said Alice, gingerly climbing on top of her seat. She squinted toward the parachute. "This angle isn't great, but it will have to do. Would you mind getting me that?"

Nathan handed up the high-resolution digital still camera Alice had indicated. "Is this some new hobby?" Karl asked her.

"You could say that," Alice said distractedly, framing his picture composition in the viewfinder. "It's pretty in the sunlight."

Which was certainly true, Nathan thought, as far as it went.

Karl drove them up to the edge of the chute. The material was made of panels of translucent white and orange. Not traditional parachute fabric, that

61

was certain. Strong and extremely lightweight, like most of the expedition's equipment, it had survived its trip and landing without any tears or rips. Standing right at the fringe of it, the thing looked gigantic. "I believe it is now time for my break," Karl announced, his feet up on the rover's dashboard. "Why don't you wrap this up while I am restoring myself?" Nathan grabbed one of his arms and Alice got the other, and together they dragged him out of his seat and planted him on the ground.

"Well, if *that* is the way you feel about it," said Karl. "I was only kidding!"

"Who would have imagined it?" Alice said. "All this time, and he actually has a sense of humor."

As they spread out along the edge of the parachute and started to roll it up, the new suits really began to prove their worth. The old rigid pressure suits didn't let you move around too freely, and bending down, in particular, wasn't something they made convenient at all. The new suits, though, were so much different that they scarcely seemed like space suits at all. More like leotards, really.

The helmets were still pretty much the same — a clear dome with its transparent gold anti-radiation shield, food and water outlets, headset and small microphone, and air supply. Below the ring that sealed the base of the helmet, though, the suit clung to Nathan's body with the tight-fitting pressure of a second skin. Well, the things weren't called "skin-suits" for nothing. The tension of the suit itself exerted the necessary counter-pressure against his body. There was no need to blow it up like a balloon so that the pressure could be provided by the air. By comparison to what they'd had to deal with before, it was almost like not wearing a space suit at all.

Sure, there was still an outer suit, too, but it was really kind of like a set of coveralls. Not your normal coveralls, though, but the latest in high-tech wear. With the old suits, the problem had been getting rid of body heat, but with the skinsuits, you had to make sure you could keep warm enough. The outer suit held the climate-control system, and the small attached chest pack had controls and instruments for everything.

The bottom line was that working in his skinsuit was a pleasure. Rolling and folding and packing, it took under two hours before they had the chute fully trussed up and lashed down to the trailer behind the rover. "We're awesome," proclaimed Nathan, standing back and viewing their handiwork with his hands on his hips. "Shall we do it again?"

As they strapped themselves back into their seats, Karl said, "I hope we don't run into much traffic. Our load is so big it's completely blocked the rearview mirror."

"Nathan could be our traffic cop," suggested Alice.

"I'm just lucky you're my friend," Nathan told her.

Their next stop came quickly into sight ahead of

them as they drove east. Even moving more slowly as Karl got the feel of the vehicle with its new bulky load, they were there within fifteen minutes.

The second parachute, which had been the one attached to Cargo Pod Three, had suffered more from its pod's descent toward the ground. "Look at this!" Alice announced as they were walking one edge toward the other. "One of these seams has almost come apart!"

It would have been impossible to fabricate a single sheet of material as large as the whole parachute. Instead, the parachute had been assembled from a patchwork of smaller pieces carefully bonded together at their edges. Alice was right. Apparently the bonding solvent and its stitch-work reinforcement hadn't been quite up to their task. Either the stress when the chute had opened had been greater than expected or the seam was weaker, or maybe both. "I guess we'll have to inspect every seam," she said with resignation. "I hope we don't miss anything."

"I hope we don't have to make this inspection right now," Karl said.

"No!" said Nathan. "No, of course not. Out here, all we have to do is roll it up and load it on the truck."

The ground under this parachute was more uneven than the place the first one had come down. There were more rocks and a few gullies and pits, too, that were concealed under the chute material until you were almost on top of them. As he stumbled again, Nathan was thinking about calling out a warning to be careful. Karl and Alice *were* careful, though, and they were both light on their feet. Nathan didn't want to start acting like a nursemaid, so he kept his mouth shut.

Then Nathan heard a yell over the radio link. A cloud of dust was rising where Alice had been. She had disappeared.

# Chapter Six

Nathan broke into a run. "Alice!" he shouted. "Are you there?"

"Go slowly!" Karl was saying to him. "If the ground is unstable you don't want to fall, too!"

Karl was right. Nathan stepped carefully. He could hear a loud hiss over his headphones, too. Not the hiss of static on the airwaves, though, but a hiss like escaping gas. There was still no Alice.

Even through the dust and dirt, what had happened was immediately clear. There was another gully just ahead, underneath the parachute. It hadn't been hidden, not exactly, although the chute material wasn't transparent enough to make out its depth or details. Alice must have thought she was still four or five feet from the edge when the ground had given way under her feet. Nathan dropped to the ground and peered over the new edge down the rockslide.

"I will hold the light and the end of the rope," Karl

said, peering down into the hole. He had detoured past the rover where he had grabbed one of the emergency kits. Nathan immediately swung his legs over the edge of the landslide and eased himself down.

There was Alice. She was on her back with one leg buried under a mound of rubble. Her left arm was twisted awkwardly beneath her. Was her helmet cracked? The outside of her visor was covered with a film of red. Nathan wiped his hand across it. "Shine the light a little toward me."

He couldn't *see* a crack, or dust jets from any pressure from an escaping air jet, either. Alice could have just been knocked unconscious by her head rebounding off the inside of her helmet. Check the helmet seals next, Nathan reminded himself, remembering the emergency drill. Okay, the seal seemed intact.

Alice's air line was punctured.

Nathan zipped open his belly pocket. He ripped a patch out of its sealed package, pulled away the backing strip, and slapped the auto-adhesive side of the patch against the torn air hose, then wrapped the rest of the patch around the curve of the hose.

The hissing stopped. The air must have been escaping from right next to Alice's transmitter microphone for it to be so loud. A person could survive a total lack of oxygen without permanent damage for at least four minutes. Alice's air had been escaping, not totally absent. She had probably been getting at least something to breathe. And it had only been a minute and a half since she'd fallen, two minutes tops, even though it seemed like much more time had passed. "Alice! Wake up!" Nathan said, grabbing her right shoulder and squeezing. He didn't want to move her. What if she had broken something? Her arm was so crooked it could easily have snapped.

Over the radio, Nathan heard a mumble that sounded like a girl's voice. He saw Alice's head move, and then behind the streaked visor her eyes opened. "You fell," Nathan told her.

Alice's face was contorted in a pained grimace. "I broke my ankle," she said.

"Can you feel your feet?" Nathan asked. "Wiggle your toes?"

"Believe me," Alice said, "I can feel my feet. There. They wiggle. Are you satisfied?"

"What about your left arm?"

He could see Alice grit her teeth even harder. "It could be that I've snapped something in it," she acknowledged.

"Let me get this stuff off your leg," Nathan said.

Working quickly, Nathan rapidly shifted the rocks off to either side. He found another rip, this time in the skinsuit's material part way up Alice's shin, and applied one of the other patches to that. Each one of them carried a personal kit of emergency gear at all times in case of just this kind of trouble. Fortunately the skinsuits had been designed with field repair in mind. They had patches for the normal skinsuit material, special patches for the helmets, and utility

68

patches for things like the air lines. They seemed to be working just as specified, too.

"I'd like to try to stand up," Alice said.

"Okay, if you say so." Leaning on Nathan's shoulder for support and keeping her bad foot off the ground, Alice levered herself up. This was one time where the low gravity was an unquestionable help. Karl kept pace with their movements from above with the light. Standing and reaching up, with Nathan supporting her across her back, Alice could get her right arm over the lip of the landslide. She was keeping her left arm propped close against her chest.

"Would you like the rope?" Karl said. "I think if I take your hands and Nathan pushes from behind, we can bring you up without further damage."

"Rope?" said Alice, her voice strained. "No, no rope — give me your one hand."

Karl braced himself and grabbed Alice's right arm, and together he and Nathan pulled and shoved her up out of the ravine. Nathan scrambled up after her.

"I feel so clumsy and stupid," Alice said.

"Let's get you back to the rover," Nathan said. "Then we'll pack up and head for the base."

"Maybe not," Alice said slowly, after a short pause.

"We've got the stretcher, if you'd rather not walk, or I can pull the rover over to here," offered Karl.

"Thank you," said Alice, "but no. Let me try my own power."

When they got her to her feet, she put an arm around each of the others' shoulders for support, and

69

they began proceeding carefully toward the vehicle. Alice hopped on her good leg, keeping her weight off the bad ankle.

"What do you mean, maybe not?" asked Karl.

"I'm not really in bad shape . . ." began Alice, panting. The fall had taken a lot of energy out of her, she was discovering. The pain was also taking its toll. Still, that was to be expected. "There are medications for pain in the medical kit. I'm not in shock. When you check them, I'm sure you'll find my vital signs are stable. I don't have any other injuries that will get worse without attention. I can wait a little while to have my ankle X-rayed and bandaged."

"You're not suggesting what I think you're suggesting," Nathan said.

"Yes, I am." They arrived at the rover. Karl and Nathan eased Alice into the backseat and arranged her crossways with her legs propped up. Karl broke out the medical kit and plugged its readout lead into the biotelemetry module built into her suit's chest pack. Every person on the expedition had received basic medical examination and first-aid training. After all, there would be many times like this one where small groups would be away from the base without a fully qualified doctor on hand. The doctor would be available by radio, of course, but they could work most effectively at a distance if the people on hand could do their own physical examination and basic diagnosis.

"It's true," Karl said after a moment. "Alice's condition appears stable." He passed one of the pain medications in through the access port low in the front of her helmet. "Her suit is serviceable."

"Even if my suit goes down," Alice added, "I could just slide into one of the sleeping bags."

The "sleeping bags" were another piece of emergency equipment. Designed to fit one, you could climb into it, seal the top after you, and pressure it; sort of like a big space suit that you couldn't walk around in. The bags were intended for use in a situation like this, where a space suit failed and couldn't be sealed up. Actually, they could be used on overnight trips, too, where you didn't want to deal with hauling around and setting up a full-scale shelter.

"Anyway," said Alice, "we're here. If we don't bring back the parachute, someone else will just have to come back and do it. If the two of you are willing to do the work by yourselves, I'm willing to wait with you."

Karl looked at her, then turned to gaze at Nathan. "What she says makes sense. If she is willing to make this sacrifice, we should do no less than to live up to it."

True, Nathan thought, but there were clear regulations for this kind of situation. The guidelines told you to return to base. What if Alice did have some problem that would get worse if they let it alone? Did Nathan have the right to gamble with her health? They'd be short-staffed now, too — suppose Karl or Nathan himself had an accident now. That could turn a minor mishap into a major problem.

On the other hand, they'd been sent out to do a job. Alice was right. If they didn't finish it, someone else would have to, or they'd have to come back and do it themselves.

"Okay," Nathan said. "Let's stay and wrap this thing up. But these are the conditions. Alice, if you even think your condition might be getting *any* worse, if you feel *anything* different, you speak up immediately. You got that?"

"Okay," Alice said.

"And you, Karl," Nathan continued. "Watch every step before you take it. If you've got any doubt about anything, don't do it. Right?"

"Very well."

"Watch *me,* too. If you see me doing anything dumb, go ahead and tell me."

"Don't worry about that," said Karl dryly.

One thing Nathan *had* to do, though, regardless of his decision. He had to report in. He tuned into the channel on his communicator. The satellite was in position to relay his transmission, so contact came quickly. Although Dr. Allen was off the ship at the moment, Tara White was on communications duty and patched her in quickly. Nathan swallowed and told her the situation.

"You're in command of your team," Dr. Allen said. "This probably wouldn't be the decision I'd make, but if you feel it's under control I won't second-guess you. Make regular reports and see me when you get

72

back."

So that was it. Nathan looked at Karl and said, "Let's do it."

# Chapter Seven

In the end, they not only brought in the parachute that had tripped up Alice, but they managed to collect the third chute as well. It had been pretty much on their route back to the ship anyway. That's why they'd laid out that particular path in the first place. Both Karl and Nathan had watched their step, assisted by an occasional warning from Alice propped up back in the vehicle. Their care paid off. Karl drove with even more watchfulness than usual and stayed on the smoothest and blandest paths he could spot to avoid jarring Alice and they made it back to the *Santa Maria* an hour before sunset.

Dr. Allen personally ran Alice through a full evaluation in the ship's sickbay. Nothing had been missed in outfitting the expedition's medical supplies. After all, the nearest referral clinic was millions of miles and the better part of a year away. *Santa Maria*'s diagnostic and care facility was the equal of any university medical center's back on

Earth, and before Alice was finished she felt as though she'd been through every test known to man.

Nathan, who had been lurking outside and popping his head in every so often to check up on their progress, had a sneaking suspicion that the extensive workup was as much for Dr. Allen's own benefit as Alice's. As much as anyone else in the crew, she had to keep up her own proficiency, and didn't have too many excuses for a free guinea pig to play on. Even with all her resources, Dr. Allen's final diagnosis was still the same.

"Sprained ankle," she told Alice and Nathan as she finished wrapping the ankle in question in elastic gauze. "You guys must especially like ankles, I think?"

Nathan winced. He'd broken his ankle on the voyage from Earth while doing a dumb stunt with his skateboard in Dr. Berger's agronomy lab.

"The ankle and a chipped radius," Dr. Allen continued to Alice. "That is one of the two long bones in your forearm. You are lucky you didn't fracture it straight through. The calcium loss from weightlessness will continue to make bones brittle for some time to come. We must all be extremely careful." She looked off into the distance for a moment. "I will speak to Earth as well. Perhaps we can tweak the food supplements." She abruptly returned her attention to Alice. "I want to see you every day, young lady, and for the present, you're confined to the ship. No running around outside!"

"Yes, ma'am," Alice said meekly.

"Good. These things can happen no matter how careful you are, but I don't want to see you doing *this* again. Understood?"

"Right."

She sent Alice off but told Nathan to wait. Nathan sank back to his stool while Dr. Allen finished entering her last few remarks into Alice's file in the central medical computer.

"That was an interesting call you made, Nathan," she said. "Deciding to stay out there instead of coming back in immediately. What was your reasoning?"

Nathan had been expecting this, so he'd already had a chance to compose his thoughts. He was fatalistic. She'd put him to work pruning carrots for the rest of his life. From the time he'd broken his ankle Nathan knew she thought he was a dope. There was no reason to be a wimp, too, though. He neatly summarized the things that had gone through his mind for Dr. Allen.

She leaned back and looked straight at him. "I believe your thought process was sound," she told him when he had finished. "You made a good decision. You were lucky, too, which is a good thing to have on your side but not a good thing to bet on. Still, you went against guidelines and you took a risk."

"Being on Mars is a risk," Nathan said. "I'm not

trying to make the problem worse, I just think there are going to be times where it'll be worth more risks. Where we'll *have* to take more risks."

"Yes," Dr. Allen said. "Just so."

If they were a family, Nathan thought, Dr. Allen was the Big Mom.

"There will be times when we'll have to try to protect the investment that's been made in us, and we may have to go out on a limb to do it. Remember, though, Nathan, it's vitally important to examine all options before making that decision. Guidelines and regulations are there for a purpose. Let's not go beyond them unless we have to."

Well, that was that. Without actually coming right out and saying it, Nathan thought as he left the room, it looked like Dr. Allen had given him a qualified vote of approval for his decision. A *qualified* one, because she'd warned him not to let it go to his head, but that was okay. He'd just been hoping to get through it without having his head chewed off. Any way you sliced it, it was a relief.

Nathan wished he had his skateboard in his hands, and a good hard surface outside to ride it on. So far, Mars didn't look like skateboard country, and he didn't exactly have a whole lot of time to unwind or goof off, either. The flip side of that was that the strain and the tension never went away. It was strange to think about traveling millions of miles, farther than any human beings had ever gone for a trip, and feeling like you needed a vacation.

He walked into The Commons and found everyone huddled around Alice. They were talking about the accident.

"It is true," Karl broke in. "It was very gracefully done. One moment she was there, the next moment she had disappeared."

"Like a magician," said Nathan, "except without the top hat. I'm going to warn you, though. Nobody else better get any ideas from this."

"Oh, you mean I can't get a day off to sit in the ship by jumping off the side of a cliff?" Lanie joked.

"You already spend more time in the ship than any of us," Noemi pointed out. "You have nothing to complain about."

"Is it my fault they can't do the important stuff on the computer without me?" said Lanie. "I'm not in the ship for a rest. I'm here to work."

"There's work," said Sergei, "and then there's *work*. If you want to be a hero of the proletariat, you have to—"

"Fall in a ditch," Ian finished for him. The Sinn Fein tattoo on his arm writhed as he made a good-natured poo-pooing gesture. "You want to know about the real world, I could tell you about some *real* work, boyo. And now instead Alice'll be hanging around here, scouting out the kitchen, grabbing the one or two interesting plates out of this bland junk we've had to eat—"

"Meal planning has not been the strongest part of this mission," Alice said. "At least we've got a good variety of seeds. When the crops come in—"

"And when's that going to be?" said Tara. "You're the plant wizard, but you won't be planting any time soon."

"Then somebody should of thought of this a long time ago," Tara stated. "How low we were going to get if all we had to eat was the same boring stuff all the time."

"I am sure they did think of it," said Sergei. "Incentive."

"Incentive?"

"Sure," Sergei expounded. "Old trick. If you want to make someone move somewhere else, you either make the other place so exciting they can't possibly stay where they are or you make people so miserable where they are that they can't wait to leave. If possible you even do both."

"Tell me about it," said Tara.

"I'm not sure I like the sound of that," Lanie said.

"It works whether you like it or not," said Sergei. "You don't like the food, but there isn't any other food until you grow it, right?"

"All I know is there better be a way to plant seeds without breaking my nails," Noemi said. "They're a mess anyway and—"

"Excuse us," the others shouted.

# Chapter Eight

It would be awhile before they had crops, that was for certain, but they were still making a lot of progress, Nathan reflected several days later. He had turned the recovered parachutes over to another work group, and they were hard at work on spreading them out, inspecting the material and the seams, and preparing them for their next role. In fact, the base had been transformed into a virtual hive of activity, with people scuttling here and there on various errands and setting up shop throughout the area on their different tasks.

Over the next few weeks, Nathan and his group were split up and trying to do a bunch of things at once.

"I hope this really pans out," Lanie told him. They were standing outside the ship near the solar panel field. Next to them was a ten-foot-tall structure that looked like a miniature oil derrick framed with light metal tubing.

"We knew we'd be on stringent water rationing," Nathan said. "The recycling system's working okay so we're not about to run out immediately."

"That recycling system should never have left the laboratory," commented Karl from his position on his knees at the base of the derrick. He was carefully adjusting the drilling head, with frequent reference to the laser-alignment instrument mounted alongside it. "The water tastes like metal and chemicals. You can tell it's been used, and we all know what it has been used *for*."

"Yeah," said Lanie. "If this thing works out, we can use the recycled waste water for the crops and start drinking fresh. If there's really any water down there."

Many of their problems came back to water, or the lack of it. As far as anyone knew, the last time there had been free water on the surface of Mars had been two billion years ago or so. Give or take as much as you reasonably could, that wasn't going to make anyone optimistic about finding some pool or stream still sitting out where it was easy to get to. At the poles, sure, there was likely water ice mixed with the frozen carbon dioxide in the shiny white polar caps that were easily apparent even from Earth through a small telescope. But they wouldn't have the resources to explore the poles anytime soon.

Actually, there probably hadn't been large bodies of water on the Martian surface even back a few billion years ago. Gen had told them that geologists speculated that at least some of the runoff channels and other remaining signs of water had been caused by the melting and escape of ice from under the surface. In fact, they thought it was likely that a layer of permafrost, soil loaded with frozen water, could be found underground all across the planet. At the poles, it might lie only an inch or two underneath the surface; the polar ice layers might even be the reservoir that fed the rest of the planet. At the equator where they were, though, how deep might this permafrost be found, if it was even there at all? If it was within tens of feet, or even a few hundred, this drill rig should be able to get access to it. If the layer was deeper than that, they would be out of luck.

"There had better be water down there, that's all I can say," Lanie commented, answering her own remark. "I've been through the computer projections. If we don't find water on site, sooner or later we're going to run out."

"Nathan," said Karl, "you have been keeping up with the reports from the other bases, correct?"

"Yep," Nathan said. The other two landing ships, *Niña* and *Pinta,* had landed in the neighborhood but not right next door, so to speak, on the philosophy that it was better not to put all their Earth-eggs in the same basket. Also, establishing a single base with four hundred inhabitants would require a lot more construction, farming, and infrastructure than spreading out into three sites, and would give them more leeway in case something went seriously wrong at one base or another. There had been regular communication among all three ships from the time they'd landed—all the way from Earth, in fact—but actual travel from one to the other would have to wait for the time being.

Each base had had its own trials and obstacles to overcome. For whatever reason, their team was the first to try to dig down to the permafrost. Nathan told them that.

"On the leading edge again, huh," grunted Lanie.

"Pioneers for hire," Nathan said. "That's us."

"Frankly," said Karl, pushing himself to his feet, "I would rather be driving something."

"It's all yours," Lanie told him, indicating the derrick. "The latest in cutting-edge technology, the Ground Boring Vehicle, Mark I. If you're ready, let's go for it!"

"Vehicle? Well, I suppose if you look at it in a particular way. Very well." Karl referred to his computer notebook, which was now plugged into the drill system's communications socket. "The batteries are fully charged, the sensors are live, so let us start!" He toggled the start sequence. The hollow-end drill began to rotate and rapidly spun up to speed, then dropped down and chewed into the ground. Behind the drill was a ten-foot aluminum cylinder the diameter of the hole in the drill bit. These cylinders, attached end to end as the drill dug further into the rock, would capture the core sample of material the drill had passed. When examined in the laboratory, the cores would give a complete cross section of geological features beneath the surface. Hopefully, one of these features would be permafrost.

The drill paused with the first core tube just protruding from the ground. Nathan helped Karl manipulate the next tube into position behind it and lock it into place. The drill was making a hole that was wider than the tube, leaving enough room for the power cables and control lines that connected the ground systems to the drill. When they had finished, Karl revved the drill back up, and again it sank down away from them.

After the third core tube had been attached and had begun to draw down into the ground, the drill suddenly throttled itself back. "Twenty-five feet," Karl said. "Between eight and nine meters."

"Is it the frost layer?" asked Nathan.

"It takes a different amount of effort to drill through different kinds of materials," Karl explained. "Whenever the drill encounters a change in the ground it is tunneling through, the power and speed requirements change. I have programmed it to stop whenever this happens so that we can carefully evaluate what is happening."

"Is it harder to drill through ice than through rock?" said Nathan. "Can't you just melt through ice?"

"The heat of the friction between the spinning drill and the surrounding material does raise the temperature," said Karl. "In ice, however, the problem is that if you melt the ice at the drill, it freezes again when the core tube tries to slip past and the tube can get locked into place. It is actually a better idea not to melt the ice in the first place. That is why the drill bit is actually refrigerated—we cool it down to make sure any ice does not melt. Now, let us just dig down a little more . . ." He delicately increased the power to the drill and let it go for another foot, then quickly shut it down.

"Okay," Karl said. "Now let us look at what we have found."

Nathan and Lanie worked with Karl to attach the topmost core tube to the winch at the top of the derrick. With the drill moving slowly in reverse and the winch pulling upward, the tube slid out of the ground. They stopped after the topmost section had emerged to disconnect it, cap the ends, and label it, and then refastened the winch cable to the next tube below it. Finally the lowest-most tube drew up into view with the drill assembly still hooked up below it. They quickly broke the tube loose and peered anxiously at the revealed end.

"Looks like we're in luck," said Lanie. Instead of the unbroken orange-and-red dirt each of the higher sections had contained, this end of the tube had streaks of clear and white stuff swirled in.

"It will need to be purified," Karl said. "It will be

85

very saline, loaded with salt, to exist this close to the surface, and you can see how it is embedded in this porous mixture of gravel and fractured rock, but I believe you are correct. It looks like ice frost to me, too."

"Okay!" said Nathan. "Way to go!" Their off-the-cuff conclusions would have to be checked in the lab, of course, but it was looking good. They would have water!

"We could dig it out," Karl was saying. "That would take a lot of time and energy, though. It would make more sense to melt the ice down where it is and just pump the water out as a liquid."

"How about a solar heater, like they use for swimming pools back home?" asked Nathan. "Set up a closed loop of tubing with liquid in it. We have sunlight to heat the liquid on the surface—all we do is pump the liquid around in a circle and it'll melt the ice underground like you said."

It turned out that they had a solar heating system on board intended for just the use Karl and Nathan had thought up. "Well, you guys know you're on the right track," Lanie said over her shoulder to them where they'd crowded up behind her at her computer station. "Nice to know somebody had their brain turned on when they packed some of our supplies, anyway."

It would take awhile to set the system up, but at least they now knew there really was water available. There would have been another way to get water, too, but it would have required a lot more power, and the machinery was turning out to be more finicky than anyone had expected. To put it plainly, it didn't work.

Ian and Gen had taken the thing on as their project. Nathan found Gen sitting cross-legged on the floor in one of the shipboard work bays, disassembled parts spread out neatly in front of him on a sheet of plastic. Ian was standing over him with his arms planted belligerently in his hips with a frustrated look on his face.

"A compressor should be a simple thing," Gen said.

Nathan lowered himself down next to Gen and tried to look at the pieces through Gen's eyes. Nathan had always been okay with mechanical things himself, but he couldn't make heads or tails of this mess. "It's supposed to process the atmosphere, right?"

"Process, yeah," said Ian. "Think of the atmosphere as a mine. When you dig down into the ground you may find valuable minerals; then you have to dig them out and refine them so they can be used. If you find the right things, you can use them as raw materials, combine them, and build other compounds. The atmosphere's the same. It could be a pretty damn rich source of materials we could use. It's good that now we know we can use the permafrost layer for our water. That means we can use the atmosphere miner to concentrate on these other resources."

He pointed at one end of the large assembly. "Before we can use it for anything, though, one crucial step has to take place. Air's drawn in through this vent, right? It's compressed using this turbine compressor." Spreading his hand, he indicated the arrangement of parts before him.

"Except it doesn't work."

"Right," Ian admitted with a grimace. On the way out from Earth he'd boasted that there wasn't a piece of equipment made he couldn't strip down and put back together better than it had started. It had actually turned out to be true. Not only that, he had a maniacal talent for improvisation, for assembling useful devices out of heaps of unrelated junk. He'd honed these skills the hard way — back on Earth he'd been headed for a career as the explosives expert for the Irish Republican Army in Belfast. It had taken leaving the Earth behind to pry him from the IRA. "It's partly my fault. I've been trying to make this bucket of garbage more efficient so that it'll use less energy. I got an idea for using the waste heat from the ship to drive the turbine, but I haven't been able to make that work yet, either. Damn it all."

"When you get it to work, what happens then?" asked Nathan.

"Thanks for the vote of confidence," said Ian. "Dr. Al-Wahab just went away muttering before you showed up. I don't think he thinks it'll ever do a thing. We'll show 'im, right, mates? *When* it works, then, like you got it, we turn to the goo-doctor here. Biology and biochemistry and all that synthesis stuff's Gen's bag, mate, not mine. 'Course, he does have that photographic memory of his. Right handy sometimes."

"For that," Gen told him, "you get U2, next time I pull my guitar out."

"Goo?" reminded Nathan. "Synthesis?"

"You know it," said Gen. "First water condenses out of the air, then carbon dioxide, then nitrogen and argon and so forth. Then we start doing chemistry. Nitrogen and the hydrogen from water can make ammonia, which we can use to fertilize and feed the crops and to power up the fuel cells. Ammonia can be turned into hydrazine, nitrogen tetroxide. We can make methane, methanol, formic acid — the basic building blocks for much of organic chemistry. And so forth."

"What about the water from the underground ice layer? Can't you use that for all this chemical synthesis?"

"That will help a lot," Gen agreed. "We still need the other ingredients, though." He adjusted his position, stretching his back, and the bright design on his suit rippled and sparkled in the sunlight.

Everyone working outside had traded their old pressure suits for the much more comfortable and convenient skinsuits. They were comfortable, there was no denying that, but they were all the same plain white color. Except for Gen's. Emblazoned across the back of his suit was the same rocket-guitar and lightning-bolt motif he'd revealed on his T-shirt. Where he'd gotten the free time to paint the design Nathan didn't know. He told Gen as much.

Gen smiled at him. "The power of will can accomplish much," he said, as though it was a proverb.

"You're doing your inscrutable number again," Nathan pointed out. "I thought you hated to play stereotypes."

"I have been doing a lot of thinking about this problem with the miner," Gen admitted. "I have been doing research, too, yes, of course, but also thinking. Sometimes when I am thinking I will help out with other work outside at the same time. Other times I stay in the ship and work with my hands so that my mind can be free. I play my guitar—with headphones, of course—but sometimes I do other things. So, you see."

Well, if it delivered results. Gen did have a memory that was photographic, as Ian had said, but in addition to its photographic side, it had turned out to be perhaps the most creative mind on the expedition. This had showed in Gen's music from the very start, but along the way it had revealed itself in the ever-increasing sophistication of his system concepts as well. Gen had come to look at engineering, whether mechanical or biological, as just another art form. "Keep it up, I guess," said Nathan, and he

90

strolled off to check up on Alice and Noemi.

In many ways, Noemi had always seemed to be the odd person out among the varied personalities of Nathan's group. On the face of it, the thought of Noemi devoting her life to space had sounded fairly absurd. A gift for pure mathematics was probably not the primary skill you'd look for in one of the first colonists to another planet, but it was downright mainstream compared to her hobbies and lifestyle back on Earth. Nathan and his mother had had each other and that was about it. There had been no money for luxuries or even some necessities, either. Nathan remembered how long he'd had to save to even buy himself his high-performance skateboard and all the pads and protectors he needed to keep from breaking his neck. Compared to his own experience, a life of wealth and privilege might as well have been something from another world.

Noemi had had all of that, and more. Her family was one of the wealthiest in Venezuela. She had never wanted for a thing, and that was particularly impressive when you realized that she had wanted an awful lot. Math may have claimed her mind but shopping had claimed her soul. Saying good-bye to glamour and fashion had hit Noemi hard, and Nathan didn't think she was over it yet. She might *never* be over it. Who knew how long it would be before they had a store on Mars, but whenever that happened, Nathan had no doubt that Noemi would be the first one in the door on its first day of business, even if it was only selling oxygen tanks or mining gear or rocks.

All of that wasn't to say that Noemi had been useless, though. Her feeling for math had given her a talent for being able to visualize the way something would look before it was built. Not only could she see in her mind how plans would translate into reality, she could tell what was wrong with them and how to make them better — more efficient, more compact, smoother in the way they would operate. When she set her mind to a problem, she had determination, too. On the voyage from Earth she'd redesigned the ship's water recycling system. The new version was awaiting its patent back on Earth.

One of the biggest planning tasks underway at the moment was laying out the greenhouse.

"Hi, Nathan," Alice said with a smile, looking up from the big screen where the greenhouse floorplan was displayed. Noemi mumbled a distracted "h'lo," too, not taking *her* eyes off the image. These days the more engrossed she was in something mathematical, the less chatty she was.

"How's your ankle?"

"Dr. Allen said it's healing incredibly fast. I should be back to normal in time for the work on the greenhouse."

Nathan looked over the floorplan. "Looks real complicated."

"This is a whole new kind of farming to get used

to," Alice told him. She leaned back in her chair and gazed back at the screen. "Back home we knew what land we had, how much seed to put in, more or less what to expect from the weather. Here we've got this tiny little patch of growing space to work with. We have to figure out what mix of which plants to put in for the best yield and most balanced diet, how much water each option will need, how much feed and nutrients, where to put the irrigation lines, how much maintenance, even how much air they'll have to have!"

"Zucchini," said Noemi. "What do you think about zucchini?"

"I hope you're not asking me," Nathan said.

"That might work," Alice said thoughtfully. "Over here, you think?" She pointed at the small growing box Noemi had highlighted.

"Yes, here," Noemi said. "Or here."

"That's good. What does it do to the beets?"

Nathan slipped away without saying good-bye. They might remember that he'd been there, but he doubted they'd seen him go or that they'd remember anything he'd said, not that he'd said much. Part of being a leader, he was starting to suspect, was knowing when to get out of the way.

As long as he was in the ship he decided to swing by and check up on Sergei. It was late in the day anyway, and there wasn't much point in getting suited up again to go back out. Sergei was sprawled on his bunk in their cabin. "So, what've you been doing on your break, guy?" Nathan said, leaning in through the door.

"Reading."

"Reading?"

Sergei stretched his leg out and wriggled his toes. "I have been working on administration tasks here on *Santa Maria,* and taking my turn on the communications boards and so on. I have been working out in the gym more also. This switch to inside ship work has its advantages. So I have been reading. We have an extremely well-equipped digital library in the computer, you know."

Most of the collection of the Library of Congress, actually, including the film and graphic arts archives, through the miracle of high-density bulk storage. "Huh," said Nathan. "What kind of stuff have you been reading? Unless you just started at the A's and are working your way along the alphabet."

"What else?" said Sergei. "Mars. You would be amazed at how much interesting fiction has been written about Mars. *War of the Worlds!* Edgar Rice Burroughs! *The Martian Chronicles.* All very fantastical, of course."

"If I was going to spend my time doing research," Nathan said, "I'd want to be reading stuff that had something to do with our real problems."

"Yes, yes, of course!" agreed Sergei. "There is much of that, too— *The Sands of Mars!* "The Martian Way!" "In the Hall of the Martian Kings!" *Icehenge,*

*Frontera, Voyage to the Red Planet.* "Green Mars." Very realistic, very interesting."

"Tell you what," said Nathan. "You can be director of historical research. You hunt this stuff up, check it out, and tell the rest of us about it. Next time we're sitting around outside in our sleeping bags around the campfire you can tell us a story."

# Chapter Nine

So work went on. Once you got past the thrill of being on another planet, of a sky that was pink and a horizon that was unnaturally close, of wearing a fancy space suit any time you had to go out the door, once you got past the neat and interesting stuff, that is, it was a job. Nathan didn't know if you could go so far as to say it was *boring*. They *were* on another planet, after all. They'd slaved, competed, and dreamed to get where they were. However, Nathan was discovering that he really hadn't had much idea of what "there" would actually be like. It sure wasn't an adventure a minute. It was more of a long-term construction site.

Of course, in his studies Nathan had discovered that most things weren't all they were cracked up to be. Thomas Edison had described genius as "ten percent inspiration and ninety percent perspiration," and many people had applied similar description to other activities. Flying was not the only pursuit characterized as "lots of sitting around punctuated by moments of pure terror." Judged by those standards, the expedition to Mars so far had been living up to form.

On the other hand, things could have been worse. They'd already had problems and dealt with them. Alice was back on her feet none the worse for the experience, and if the third cargo pod was out of their grasp, well . . . they'd been managing to get along without it. They'd probably have more problems. You had to *expect* problems. But they'd handle the new problems, too. When you got right down to it, how much worse would things get, anyway?

This wasn't to say that the slow construction work of building their settlement was the same from each day to the next, either. Sooner than Nathan had anticipated, a big day had arrived. It was time to put up the greenhouse.

Everyone was up and out early, as usual, but today virtually the whole shipload of young colonists would be participating in the same job in one way or another. It was their biggest challenge yet.

Nathan stopped on his way over from the ship and looked ahead at the crater. The scene was lit by the rising sun at his back, just now clear of the horizon. The translucent white of the folded parachute material along the crater's edge seemed to glow against the reds and oranges of the rust-laden Martial soil. It was clearly evident that final preparations had been going on for the last several days.

Not only were there the parachute sections, Nathan could see the long coiled lengths of cable stacked at regular intervals next to the piles of fabric. Attached through a turnbuckle and a clamp to one end of each coil of cord, a sturdy spike was firmly embedded in the ground.

The edge of the crater itself had also been attacked by the advance preparation team. Crumbly sections of rock and gravel had been evened out or carted away or used to fill cracks. Using the Martian soil as the main ingredient combined with an acrylic paste, the settlers had been making concrete and bricks, too, and both had been applied liberally to shore up a few unstable areas and to seal the coarser gravel fill.

Numbered flags had been planted next to each spiked cable. The numbers went up as you walked clockwise around the crater. With his small band of friends trailing behind him, Nathan led the way off to the right. Around them, other teams were making their way to and fro, peering at the numbers to find their own places. Poised at the very edge of the crater's lip and dug down into it as they passed was a boxy structure that looked like a small house trailer. "What is that?" Karl asked, pointing.

"The airlock," said Alice. "See the sealed doors?" There were several sets of doors, actually, both person-size ones and a large hatch big enough to fit one of the rovers as well.

"Is there only the one airlock?" Nathan wondered.

"Well, we only brought enough materials to build one initially. When we're all set up and running and we can take apart the *Santa Maria*, we can add the big airlock assembly from the ship here, too."

"We have arrived, I believe," said Sergei. "Isn't our first position number 53?"

It was indeed. "Sergei, why don't you take that one," Nathan said. "Alice, you're next with 54, then me, then Noemi, Karl, Lanie, and Gen. Careful sliding over the parachute material."

"We have been through this in the briefing, Nathan," Karl reminded him. "You don't have to remind us of every little detail."

"All right, all right," said Nathan. "Just watch your footing going down the slope. Even if you do have the ropes—"

"Okay, Mom," Lanie said. "We've got it, Mom." She got a general round of chuckles out of that remark.

"Okay," said Nathan. "I guess I deserve that. I'll keep my mouth shut."

They climbed gingerly over the folded parachute fabric and started down, their cables in hand. There was a definite lip on the edge of the crater, true, and the slope inside was reasonably steep just inside it, but a crew had been busy with one of the rovers and a bulldozer blade creating flat terraces and convenient ramps between them. Here and there ladders had been hung as well, and since the lower gravity made it possible to navigate a steeper slope without falling than would have been possible on Earth, the danger of an accident had been pretty much reduced, as long as people paid attention to what they were doing.

People were now walking inward toward the center of the crater from halfway around its edge. "It's almost like a dance," Noemi said. "Sort of a weird dance, though."

"Don't give Gen any ideas," Sergei implored.

"Now that you mention it . . ." broke in Gen himself.

"Careful there, Number 22!" said Ian's voice. He was one of the people coordinating this job. He was behind them, still up on the crater lip, where he could look over everyone's movements and plot them against the desired computer profile. "Like a bloody Maypole," he muttered, "that's what this lot is."

"I still don't see why all this is necessary," said Noemi. "Couldn't they just throw the ropes across the crater? Or even shoot them out of airguns, or attached to darts or something like that."

"Uh," said Nathan.

Alice rescued him. "Actually you're right, there were any number of ways this job could have been done. The greenhouse team decided this one was best for several reasons. It's fastest, for one, and the simplest, too, when you get right down to it. The most important reason, though, is just what you said before."

"I did?" Noemi said. "A dance?"

"Well, sort of like a dance, anyway. An excuse to get everybody together and have them pitch in on the same project."

"Like a barn-raising," said Nathan. "Out on the frontier or in a farming community, say, when somebody was going to put up a new barn or a farmhouse or a silo or something like that, all the neighbors would come over and help them out. They'd start early in the morning and do it all in one or two days, and then they'd have a big party and dance until the middle of the night."

"Exactly," Alice agreed. "In farming country, everyone's pretty isolated off in their farmhouse in the middle of all their land, so you have to have a special excuse to get together with your neighbors."

"It has been much the same with us," said Sergei, jumping down from one terrace to the next lower down. They were getting close to the center of the crater now. "We have been so busy with our individual tasks and problems we have scarcely seen each other."

Ahead of them was a curving line of people who had reached the center first. They were waiting next to each other while Ian called the number of their ropes in the correct order. "Number 40," he said. "Now Number 25." The ropes had to be woven together in a particular sequence in order to give maximum support to the parachute material. All this had been set up on the computer. One by one the members of Nathan's group were called, and they spread out across the other side of the crater, now walking ground that sloped up rather than down; Nathan discovered that less of the ground on this side had been graded into terraces, too.

"Head to your left, 55," said Ian. That was Nathan! He stopped in place and extended one arm ahead of him, then began turning slowly to the left. "There," Ian told him. "That's the direction!"

Nathan set out in the new direction. When they were finished, the rope would snake and intertwine, not just loop directly over the center of the crater. As a result, cables that started next to each other where they attached on one end would end up some distance away at their termination.

It took a while, but each person finally managed to find their number at the far side of the crater. The same type of clamp, turnbuckle, and spike arrangement was already in place. After locking the end of his cable into place, Nathan cast a glance over the edge of the crater at the work they'd already done. It didn't look like a greenhouse. In fact, it didn't look like much of anything, except maybe like a giant net that somebody had dropped over a big hole in the ground. It really looked like a mess.

The construction team seemed to know what they were doing, though; Ian certainly did. Nathan joined up with the crowd trudging back along the rim of the crater to their original starting positions. He thought he recognized the person ahead of him — sure he did. "So what do you think, Alice?" he asked her.

"Where are you? — Oh! there you are." She paused and let him come up. Nathan saw her dial up one of the short-range conversation channels on her radio and he followed suit.

They walked again, side by side. "I'm excited," Alice admitted. "Pretty soon we'll be able to take the plants out of the ship into the greenhouse, where they'll really have room to grow! We'll be able to plant seeds! It'll be almost like a real farm. Like a farm back home." Her voice drooped and trailed off.

"I miss home, too," Nathan said after a moment. "There's been so much to do, I've been so busy, there's been almost no time to think about *anything* more than the next task. But I do think about it, and, well . . ."

"I know," said Alice. "We're tough, we'll make it."

"Of course we're tough. Sometimes I just kind of wish I didn't have to be so tough all the time."

"Maybe you don't have to. Oh, well, here we are."

And so they were. Nathan was surprised he'd said what he'd just said. Until the words had come out, he hadn't even realized part of him had been thinking that way. That was the good thing about having a friend like Alice. He didn't have to worry about what he said to her. She took him seriously when that's what he needed. He tried to do the same for her, too.

"Let's get this show on the road, boss-man," Gen said suddenly, clapping him on the back. Even when you were talking on one of the conversation channels, it was standard practice to leave your main communication channel open so you could listen but not transmit. With a guilty start, Nathan switched back to the work channel and tried to get his mind back on the job.

The folded length of parachute material at the edge of the crater was now underneath the rope netting. They now had to carefully unfold the fabric and stretch it all the way across the crater and anchor it to the other side. While they worked, they would have to keep the material from scraping across the ground or against the ropes, which could weaken or tear it.

Even with more than a hundred people working, it was afternoon before they had this part of the job finished. A glistening whitish carpet now stretched across the crater's floor underneath the cable netting. The carpet was secured all the way around in a long mounting strip bolted directly into the rock. Soft plastic moldings between the mounting strip and the rock and between the parachute material and the strip would keep it airtight. Dr. Allen had declared a holiday for the rest of the afternoon, and people were already streaming back to the ship. Across the crater from Nathan, though, Ian and his construction-team mates were checking the seals around the airlock and setting up the pumping system.

Ian and Gen had finally gotten their compressor working two days earlier and the atmosphere miner was busily starting to refine materials from the gases of the air. Lanie and Karl's exploratory water well, too, had quickly yielded to a full-scale effort. A system of pipes had been bored down into the permafrost layer. One pipe in each set ran to a closed-loop solar heater on the surface. Liquid heated by the sun would circulate down into the ice layer and melt the ice around it. This melted water would then be pumped out by the other pipes. *Santa Maria*'s empty fuel tanks had been pressed into service as water tanks, but some of the water was being diverted to a processor tank to be broken down into hydrogen and oxygen. This oxygen would now be mixed with refined nitrogen and carbon dioxide from the Martian atmosphere to form the air inside the greenhouse.

"You want to head in now?" Nathan asked Alice. The other team members were on their own way back to the ship, but Alice had been waiting by the edge of the crater.

"Not yet. You go on if you want."

"No," said Nathan. "I'll wait a while longer, too. What are we waiting for?"

"That!" Alice's voice was animated and excited again. She pointed. Next to the airlock, a small section of fabric had suddenly begun to ripple. The ripple spread slowly. Behind it, though, a low bulge began to rise, as though a giant worm was leisurely starting to tunnel underneath the carpet. Ian had turned on the pumps and opened the gas valves. The greenhouse tent was beginning to rise.

"Do you want to stay until the dome is completely inflated?" Nathan asked.

"No," Alice said reluctantly. "It won't be done until middle of the day tomorrow. But I can hardly wait to see what it looks like."

"Me, too." Of course, they *had* seen computer-generated pictures of what it would look like, Nathan thought, so their visualization wasn't completely a question of imagination. A low dome of parachute material would arch across the top of the crater, held in place by the cable netting on top of it. No internal columns or pylons would be required. The increased air pressure inside would hold the material tight. The pressure inside would only be about one-third the pressure at sea level on Earth, but it would be enough to allow people to work inside with only oxygen masks—no suits! Even more importantly, the air should allow their crops to thrive.

"Okay, I've seen it start," said Alice. "Let's go inside. Maybe I'll come out again later and have another look."

They strolled together away from the crater. "It's a pretty big step," said Nathan. "Feels like we're really getting somewhere."

"Not bad," Alice agreed. "It's nothing compared to what we'll be able to do someday, though. Terraforming, I mean."

Terraforming was the process of converting the hostile environment of another planet to a comfortable one like Earth's. A few good-size comets would be crashed into the planet, releasing the water bound up in their icy cores. Giant mirrors in orbit and then the greenhouse effect would be set into motion to bring up the surface temperature. Genetically engineered microbes and plants would convert carbon dioxide into oxygen. First small oases in deep craters and later portions of the whole surface would have running water and breathable air. "But a journey of a thousand miles begins with a single step," he said.

"Are you turning into a philosopher?"

"I stole that line," Nathan admitted, "from Gen."

# Chapter Ten

The only place in the settlement where you couldn't see the greenhouse dome that now covered their crater was from behind the *Santa Maria*. It sure did make a statement. The Martians were here to stay.

The greenhouse wasn't the only new feature of the landscape, either. The dirt and rock that had been dug up from all the grading and excavating was being turned into bricks, and the bricks were starting to rise into buildings. "Kind of mundane, isn't it," Nathan commented.

"How so?" asked Sergei, who was taking a turn on one of the construction teams. It was break time at the moment.

Nathan had been working hard himself. He was a team leader, though, and that gave him the responsibility for keeping track of his people, making sure they were okay and finding out if they had any complaints or problems he could help them out with. Actually, Nathan thought the most important part of the job was just keeping their spirits up and making sure they still felt part of the group. He had one day a week reserved in his own work schedule to use just for walking around.

"I mean," he said, "here we are traveling to another planet, and are we getting gleaming metal? New plastics? No, we're using *bricks,* of all things."

"It's practical," Sergei pointed out. "Every use we can make of the local resources is that much more material we don't have to have shipped from Earth."

"I know," said Nathan. "I know. I'm not *against* bricks. Bricks are fine with me. I just think it's a little funny, that's all."

"Stay with me and lift a few thousand," Sergei said darkly. *"Then* see how funny you think bricks are."

"They're really coming along, though. Look at this." Nathan was gazing over the construction site. Four rectangular buildings were going up in this phase of construction. The foundations had been dug down into the ground to the height of a person. Using Martian concrete, slabs and retaining walls had been poured. The brick structures were rising on top of the concrete. The buildings would serve as barracks initially, giving people the opportunity to spread out from the cramped quarters of the ship. Eventually each person would get a room to themselves, but that goal was a lot of building away.

"Yes," said Sergei, "and when we are finished we get to bury all this again. I never thought so much of exploring a new planet would involve moving dirt."

"Maybe you'll be in line to run the bulldozer," Nathan suggested. A layer of dirt would protect against the radiation hazards of the solar flares that were sure to strike sooner or later. Talk about mundane, though. As if brick wasn't ordinary enough, they were going to end up living in a bunch of big mole tunnels!

One of the rovers hummed past next to them. Karl gave them a brief wave from the driver's seat as it drove by down the "street." That probably *was* how streets got started, Nathan reflected. It was a straight line from the assembly area next to *Santa Maria* to the airlock on the greenhouse. Gazing after Karl, Sergei said, "If I am to do anything with that vehicle, I will need more time to practice my driving skills."

"You've had as much time as anyone, haven't you?"

"As anyone but Karl."

It was true. Karl had been hogging the vehicle assignments. "I'll speak to him," Nathan promised.

"Thank you," said Sergei, pushing himself to his feet. "Now, it is time to return to work. The labor of the strong for the good of the State."

"Are you going to start that again."

"But it sounds so good," Sergei said, his face

110

moping in an exaggerated pout. Then he winked, made a wry face at himself, and slapped Nathan on the back. "See you later, my friend."

"You got it," said Nathan. He turned and followed Karl and the rover up the street. The big airlock door was just closing behind the rover up ahead. When Nathan reached the greenhouse, he let himself in through the smaller person-size airlock next to the big one. Once the airlock had pressurized itself to match the conditions inside the greenhouse, the inside door opened for him.

Just outside the hatch was a rack containing a mixture of helmets, skinsuits, and oxygen masks; underneath, a long line of oxygen tanks were charging. Nathan held his breath, broke the seal on his helmet, and exchanged it for a mask, which he plugged into a fresh oxygen tank, its indicator showing all green. The mask was specially designed to allow the wearer to speak through a small amplifier near the mouth. Then he turned to survey the garden spread out ahead of him.

Well, it wasn't *that* much of a garden, really, or at least not yet, anyway. Only a long wedge partway down the nearest slope was green. That was where the plants from the ship had been going in. The surrounding sections were being watered, though, and rows of stakes here and there showed where seeds were already in the ground. Knots of people around the greenhouse were intent on their tasks. Karl pulled the rover to a halt next to a plot with fresh irrigation tubing and several people converged on it. When unzipped, a pressurized bag covering the trailer revealed more trays of plants from the ship.

"So what do you think?" said a voice at his side.

"Yow!" Nathan yelped. It was Alice. "Oh, hi. I didn't even hear you come up."

"When you've just taken your helmet off it can take a minute or two to orient yourself," she explained. "The pressure's only a third of normal so sound carries differently. You're right on time, I see."

"Well, heck, if you're gonna do a job, you might as well do it right."

"My sentiments exactly. So what *do* you think?"

"There's a lot of room to grow," Nathan said cautiously.

"I see I'd better give you the tour first, then get your evaluation later. Step this way."

Nathan followed her along a path that threaded its way down the terraces. "First stop," Alice said, indicating an empty plot of turned earth slightly soggy with moisture from the drip irrigation system. "Those will be radishes. I hope you like radishes. We're going to have a lot of radishes." She took a quick glance at Nathan to gauge his reaction, and immediately broke up in laughter. His face had screwed itself up like an infant confronted by its first green leafy vegetable.

"I hate radishes," said Nathan. "I didn't travel millions of miles to eat radishes."

"It's better than algae and bacteria, take it from me."

*Yuch*, Nathan thought. "I guess it would be, at that. But if there's one thing the planners for this project never had their finger on from the very first day, it was food. They gave us goop back on Earth and that's all they've sent us with to eat here. Now *that's* depressing."

The crater *was* starting to look less like a barren patch of lifeless desert and more like a garden, that was certainly true, although not like any garden he'd ever seen on Earth, of course. Sunlight shone through the parachute material suspended across the open mouth of the crater almost fifty feet above their heads, with the supporting cable netting outside casting dark, shadowed lines across it. The two of them were standing about halfway out from the center of the crater. Around them, the work that had been done to the ground was clearly apparent. Taking advantage of the natural slope of the crater basin, the ground had been leveled in a series of terraces like long steps leading up, arranged around each other like the circles on a bull's-eye. From where they were standing through to the center of the crater, however, the ground was flat and regular. Up above them, a new group of people came through the airlock with one of the smaller hydroponic trays from the ship, unzipped its pressure bag, and began to carefully maneuver its dolly down the ramp. Dr. Ari Berger, the Israeli chief agronomist, came through with it and raised a hand in greeting to Alice.

"Actually, there aren't really *that* many radishes," Alice admitted with a smile, waving back at Dr. Berger. "A long time ago, some researchers thought radishes would be the most efficient crop to grow in these conditions, but it turned out there were a lot more options than that. I think people set out to disprove the radish idea because so many of them didn't like radishes, either."

"Good for them!" Nathan said. He was looking closely at the raked-over ground. Some of the plots had dirt in long shallow growing boxes; others, like the radish zone, were just densely packed furrows in the bleached-orange soil cut across by the hydroponic irrigation pipes snaking their way along the ground. He didn't see radishes, though, or the slightest sprig or sprout of green. Well, they'd only started putting the seeds in a few days ago.

"Psychologically speaking," said Alice, "it's pretty important when you think about it. It's just the reason you pointed out—exploring and settling Mars is challenge enough all by itself. Making things worse by giving us food we hate, and without much variety, would only add to the trouble. If you're out there conquering a planet, working to exhaustion all the time, and all you have to look forward to for dinner is your algae with a side order of radishes . . ."

"Maybe a week of that and I'd revolt," Nathan agreed. "Don't get me wrong, I know algae are our friends, recycling wastes and helping with the air and all that, but I just couldn't take them on my plate. Not for long, anyway."

"So how about corn?" A new voice said from behind. It was Tara White. "You like corn? We'll have corn, too — not much initially, but enough for treats. Soybeans, sugar beets, wheat, lettuce, onions, potatoes, some herbs. Peanuts. All high-yield, high-protein variants, of course, and some of them had to be tweaked to like the air and the new pressure." It was okay for the plants, which were fairly flexible when it came right down to it, and it let people work inside without even the skinsuits. They still needed those oxygen masks, though. "Rice — rice is great, really, since even on Earth it grows hydroponically. All those rice paddies, you know. Pineapples! They work the swing shift — take in carbon dioxide at night, give off oxygen during the day. And when we fill up the ground level, we'll start putting up more racks and platforms and mirrors to make sure the lower levels can still get sunlight. It'll be terrific!"

Well, okay, Nathan thought. He liked to eat as much as the next guy, and he sure liked a variety more than the same thing all the time, and he didn't mind the vegetarian diet. It *was* healthy, after all. The algae and bacteria and plants and vegetables would help them build toward a closed ecology,

115

too. They'd absorb the carbon dioxide that people exhaled, and other waste products, too, and give off oxygen for people to breathe. In fact, the plants had all the carbon dioxide their little vegetable hearts desired. The atmosphere was loaded with it.

Still, Nathan couldn't get really excited about farming. Nothing like Alice, and now Tara, for sure. They were going on about how they'd grind up the parts of the plants that people couldn't eat and let vats of yeast convert them to sugar. It was a far cry from tending sheep on New Zealand, but if you farmed it or herded it or tilled it, Alice was the person you'd call. She was not only good at it, it was what she was, what she loved. You couldn't stand with her in the middle of her garden and not feel it. Even a city kid like Tara got the "grow fever" from her.

"What are those guys doing over there?" Nathan asked. Across the crater floor, one of the groups of people scattered around them on their various tasks were shoveling soil into what looked like a small cement mixer.

Alice followed his pointing finger. "Oh, that's the washer," she said. "The soil's pretty good for growing, actually, but it starts out loaded with salt; sulfuric acid, too. We've got to wash that stuff out before we can use it. Of course, once the toxic ingredients have been separated out, we can use *them,* too."

Nathan was starting to think they could use *every-*

116

*thing.* If there was some scrap of material or some waste byproduct nobody had come up with a use for, all they had to do was store it off on the side somewhere. Gen or maybe Ian or Karl would get around to it eventually.

"What about those?" They looked like medium-size beachballs, a couple dozen of them, just scattered around on the ground.

Tara grimaced. "They're supposed to be protection against leaks. If we get a hole in the fabric dome top and the air starts to rush out, the ball-things are supposed to get sucked up to the hole. They're made out of patch material and they're sticky, so the idea is for them to plaster themselves over the break and seal it off. Really, it sounds kind of weird to me."

"If we're lucky, we won't have to find out. How much more do you have to do before all the crops are in?"

"It's an ongoing job, you know," Alice reminded him. "We've been doing pretty well already, though. About another two weeks and the whole first crop should be in the ground. With the high-yield fast-growth varieties we're planting, we should be able to start harvesting a month or so after that. We'll rotate the planting and harvests so there's always some part of the crop ready to be harvested."

Alice sure knew her stuff, Nathan reflected. But then, each one of them did. There were no dead-weight people on Mars. Everyone had to do his or her part.

"Why don't you plan to come back out here in another couple weeks?" Alice suggested. "Should be a lot more to see then. I mean, you could come before that, too. Always glad to have you, but, you know —"

"I got it," said Nathan. Alice didn't usually get flustered. *Was* she flustered? "Two weeks. Sounds like fun. It's a date." A date? Well, not a *date* date. He started to tell her that, but then stopped himself. Now *he* was the one who was flustered. The two of them were just friends, like brother-and-sister kind of friends. She wouldn't want a date any more than he would.

She didn't seem unhappy with the idea, though.

For that matter, neither was he.

But what about Lisette? Nathan didn't want to get himself in the same mess Sergei was so good at. Only Sergei's good looks and sparkling personality had let him get away with juggling girls in what was frankly kind of an insensitive manner. There was no way Nathan thought he could pull off the same stunt. He didn't want to, either. He didn't want to hurt anybody. That included himself, too.

But Nathan suddenly realized how long it had been since he'd really been around Lisette. Certainly it had been a long time since they'd been *alone*. They hadn't been avoiding each other, it was just that their work assignments had taken them off in different directions, and everybody was so tired at the end of the day that there hadn't been much energy left for socializing.

"Mars to Nathan," Alice was saying. "Is anybody in there?"

"Huh? Oh, yeah, right, sure. I'm okay. Just spaced out for a second there, I guess."

"On your way, then," she said. "Some of us have work to do around here."

Alice quickly walked toward the pile of empty plant containers that Tara had begun loading into a cart.

# Chapter Eleven

Nathan took his turn with the bricklaying, helped put down pipe for the water system, stayed up late a few times to watch the crisp black night sky, hung out with the gang. Still, for some reason it felt a little bit like his birthday when he got up on the day he was scheduled to drop by the greenhouse again.

Nathan was even whistling a little as he left Gen and Ian, who were tinkering with the atmosphere miner again. He'd turned his microphone off. He wasn't crazy enough to broadcast something as dopey as *whistling*, of all things. He'd never hear the end of it. Many of them had taken to doing stuff with their transmitters off. Occasionally you'd hear a snatch of whatever they were singing or playing when someone would trigger their transmitter on without turning their sound system off first quickly enough. Karl was listening to opera, Nathan knew, working his way through all this singing in French and Italian, and this heavy German stuff, something called The Ring that seemed to go on forever. If you gave Karl half a chance, he'd try to tell you about it, too. Gen kept busy playing tunes on his intraship radio station SNAP.

Noemi, of all people, had been showing more of an interest in Gen's musical tastes, too. Or was she showing more of an interest in *Gen?* Nathan wasn't going to pry. If something was going to happen, it was going to happen.

Of course, he was sometimes the last person to find out interesting things, he'd noticed.

None of that was particularly bothering him at the moment, though. It was a fine day. The weather was its typical clear and bright self, with some of those wispy clouds shooting past overhead on their way north. Actually, they were shooting past a lot faster than usual. He dialed in the main com channel. "*Santa Maria?* What's the weather report? Looks like the clouds are moving quicker than normal."

The com person turned out to be Tara White. "Nathan? They're watching it, trying to get a better view with the satellite. There's some kind of atmospheric disturbance south of us."

"A storm?"

"Maybe. There is some dust kicking up. I'll let you know."

"Okay," Nathan said. "Thanks, Tara." He clicked off. There he was at the greenhouse entry, anyway.

Inside was a whole new picture. And Alice—she was right there again, waiting for him. "Are those all plants from the ship?" he asked. "I never realized there were so many of them."

"That's all of them," Alice said proudly.

"Look at all that green! Wow."

"Look at this, too." Alice led him on another tour. Not only was there a lot more land covered by full-scale growing stuff, the seeds that had been planted only two or three weeks before were vigorously sending up their own shoots as well. Only a third of the crater floor was under cultivation, if that much, but that was still quite a tidy expanse of land.

"This is really something!" Nathan exclaimed. "It's not much like Kansas, but in a way it sort of is."

"I feel the same way," she told him. "When you get down to it, crops are still crops. A lot of the crops are the same as I was used to back home, too. New Zealand, I mean." She looked up at the parachute dome. It seemed darker than usual. "Is it going to rain or something?"

He flipped on the com channel again. "Tara? What's the situation out there?"

"Getting some dust in the air. The command team's meeting on it now. This could be a real dust storm."

Nathan and Alice exchanged glances. One of the scientific objectives of their stay on Mars was to try to learn how to predict the Martian weather. So far, they hadn't had very much weather to practice on.

In the future, a widespread network of meteorological instruments would be set in place around the planet. At the moment, though, their coverage was still restricted to the areas around the landing sites and the pictures and sensors of the orbiting satellites.

The expedition had routinely been holding emergency drills of various types. There were individual drills, what to do if your suit got torn or your air supply conked out or your helmet cracked, that sort of thing. There were larger scale drills—what if the compartment you were in or the *ship* sprung a leak, what if there was an explosion in the fuel cells. They'd had a few significant injuries, too—Alice's, of course, and a general mix of sprains and contusions, and one person had actually broken her leg. A few people were allergic to some of the plants, but no one had gotten sick with as much as a cold. They hadn't brought any germs with them from Earth, after all, and as far as they could tell there weren't any new ones waiting for them on Mars. But those had been drills and routine medical care. Here there might be something *real*.

"Dr. Allen is coming in," said Tara. "I think—yes, she wants the mike."

Nathan's radio clicked over to the priority override channel. From the ship, Tara had switched on their emergency broadcast system. It would interrupt everyone's ongoing conversations and automatically switch them to the priority channel. In the greenhouse, where people often worked with their suits open and their suit backpacks left in the racks by the airlock, there was a public-address system, too. Its speakers crackled into life.

"This is Dr. Allen. As you may already have noticed, a large dust storm is building in the vicinity of our camp. Since this is the first such storm we will have experienced, we will deal with it by the book. I am calling a Level One Alert. As you know, this means drop whatever you are doing, secure any necessary equipment according to plan, and return to the ship immediately. That means now."

Alice cast an agonized look around the greenhouse. Everyone around the crater had straightened up to listen to Dr. Allen over the loudspeakers, and now they were streaming toward the airlock, leaving their tools where they had been working.

"There's nothing you can do here," Nathan said. "Everything should be fine, and if it isn't, well . . . there won't be anything you can do while it's happening, anyway. Come on, let's go."

"I could cover the plants," Alice said. "I could—"

"No, you can't." Nathan saw Dr. Berger walking rapidly past them and flagged him down.

"I believe I know what the problem is, yes?" he said. "My talented young apprentice thinks she should stay with the plants. Is that not so?"

"How did you know?" asked Nathan.

"Because I know Alice. Come. Our place is in the ship."

Between Nathan's hand on her arm and Dr. Berger's words, they got Alice moving. Both airlocks were cycling when they reached the exit. Overhead, the sky through the dome was definitely darker, and occasional shudders ran across the dome material itself. When they emerged from the big airlock with the last remaining group, the scene was different from any they had yet seen on Mars.

Instead of pink, the sky had gone a murky orange. They could easily see the ship and the other structures around the site, although they were not as sharp as usual. The hills beyond had pretty much faded from view, however. From every direction, people were streaming toward the ship. Dr. Allen would be happy. No one was wasting time.

In the several minutes it took them to reach the *Santa Maria* airlock, Nathan thought it had gotten even darker. "Am I imagining it or is it getting worse?" he muttered.

"Look behind you," said Dr. Berger.

Nathan turned. The white of the dome surface that usually stood out against the landscape was now the red of Martian soil. Enough dust had already settled on the dome to cover it completely.

The line for the airlock shrunk rapidly. No one wanted to hang around outside. If they were lucky, there shouldn't be much to worry about, really. The dust particles were very fine and might choke machinery, but there wasn't much machinery out where the dust could get to it. The rovers were sealed in

125

their garages, the atmosphere miner had its own protective bags, and people were bringing other sensitive tools and equipment into the ship with them. Martian winds could be fast and strong, but since the atmosphere was so much thinner than Earth's, the punch a wind would pack would be a lot smaller as well. The colony's structures had been built with the expected strength of the winds in mind.

That had all been calculation, though. This would be the first real-world test. Mars was about to let them all know what it thought of their plans and calculations.

Once inside the ship, Nathan and Alice logged in and hurried toward The Commons. Most everyone in the crew was already there. The monitors and speakers were relaying the situation from the command deck, where Dr. Allen and the crisis team were themselves taking up all the available space.

For a crisis, it was more of a bust.

Not much happened. The camera view from outside got darker. Wind speed picked up, whipping clouds of dust along with it. People gradually drifted away from The Commons as time went on and nothing new came up to get excited about.

"This is *boring*," Noemi said after a while.

"You think this is bad, just wait for one of the *big* ones," Gen told her. Almost every year, Mars experienced dust storms that covered the entire planet and lasted for months. It was the wrong season for one that large, fortunately. This storm was strictly local. It was hitting *Niña* and *Pinta* as well, but the heaviest portion seemed to be passing right over the *Santa María* settlement.

"Something's happening," Alice said. She'd been the only one still paying rapt attention to the screens. The tone of conversation in the command center had changed. There was more tension, and they were paying particular attention to one set of readings.

"The solar panels?" asked Sergei. The output of the panels had already dropped almost to nothing. The amount of sunlight blocked by the storm was only part of the reason — the panels themselves had also been covered by dunes of dust.

"Not the panels," Alice said, her voice sick. "It's the greenhouse. I'm sure it's the greenhouse."

# Chapter Twelve

Unfortunately Alice had been right. Under the buffeting of the wind itself and the scouring action of the dust particles, one of the seams in the parachute material that made up the surface of the greenhouse dome had let go. Even if someone had been inside, there would have been no way to stop it. The seam was too high off the ground. As it was, they were only able to watch it happen from the remote cameras, pressure gauges, and other instruments inside the greenhouse.

The air inside the greenhouse had begun to rush out, propelled by the difference in pressure. Beachballs had lifted into the air and had plastered themselves against the gap, but it was too wide for them to completely bridge. The beachball patches were designed for a single puncture here or there, anyway, not a thirty-foot-long tear. The parachutes had been made of a special rip-stop Kevlar and nylon material, and the seams had all been inspected.

But it had happened. The rapid decompression had not only lifted beachballs, it had lifted everything else that hadn't been nailed down. Plants, irrigation tubing, seedlings, the hydroponic trays—it was a mess. Not much stuff had actually escaped out of the hole. No, instead it had just splattered onto the interior of the slowly subsiding dome, and then just piled up on the crater floor in a giant mash of trash.

Two days later, the storm had finally blown itself out. People had spilled out of the ship and were wandering around in a daze. Nathan's gang had come out of the airlock together, splitting up to check their different areas. Nathan was following the dejected figure of Alice. Her shoulders were slumped in despair as she trudged along. She was more depressed than Nathan had ever seen her. Probably more depressed than he had ever seen *anybody*.

Everything was covered with dust. Everything was the red color of everything else—the ship, the brick buildings under construction, the vehicle garages. The mounds of the collapsed greenhouse dome. *Inside* the collapsed greenhouse dome.

"Everything's dead in there," Alice whispered. "All the plants, all the seedlings. Everything's gone."

Ian and two others were clambering carefully along the fabric dome surface toward the ripped seam. "They'll fix it," Nathan pointed out. "They'll check everything, reinforce all the seams. This should never happen again."

"But don't you see, Nathan—the live plants we brought from Earth, the plants from *Santa Maria*—they're gone. *Gone!* And the seeds, most of our seeds . . ."

"Can't we gather them up and replant them?"

"Maybe some," she said sadly. "But the dust got into everything. Dust is not just dirt. It's still got the salt, the sulfuric acid, all the toxic things we had to wash out of the soil before we could use it. Now the soil's been poisoned again, and all the crops that were in it."

"This doesn't sound good." That was all Nathan could think of to say.

It wasn't good at all.

As soon as the dimensions of the problem started to become clear, the settlement went into overdrive. People were up around the clock. Every input slot into the computers was loaded. If the computers had been built to spew steam out of their joints or drip oil on the deck or otherwise graphically act out how overworked they were, the floors would have been awash and the air filled with vapor. They weren't, of course, and so the banks of solid-state devices kept pace with the demands, reliably churning and crunching and feeding back the same answers, no matter how cleverly the questions were posed.

They were in trouble.

They still had their power from the solar-cell array, now that the panels had been swept clear of dust. They still had their water coming up out of the permafrost layer, and some of the water could be broken down to provide oxygen. Various chemicals and compounds were coming from the atmosphere miners. The crater dome could be repaired and resealed. Losing the air from under the dome would set them back, but it, too, could gradually be replaced. Even the water from the hydroponic tanks that hadn't splattered and boiled away in the low pressure could be cleaned and filtered and reused, maybe, if they were lucky. Regenerating these resources would take time and would stretch their supplies and their endurance close to the limit, but when it came right down to it they could live through it.

The big problem was food.

Food had always been something of a gamble. All three cargo pods had been packed redundantly, with each one carrying duplicates of the essential equipment and supplies on the others. Ideally, the planners would have liked to make it possible for each base to survive on the contents of any single pod. When the size of the expedition had grown as large as it actually had, though, that goal had become impossible. Under the plan they had gone with, each of the three mother ships would require two of its three pods just to break even. For each ship, the third pod was the reserve.

*Santa Maria*'s third pod, of course, was sitting somewhere up on the Tharsis bulge almost a thousand miles away, with no way to bring its contents back even if they could get there in the first place. Getting there was no trivial matter, either. The expedition had never planned to make such long trips this early in their stay. The problems of getting established and stabilizing the settlement had a much higher priority.

True, there were worse places the pod could have come down; atop Olympus Mons, for example. If it had touched down on Olympus Mons, it wouldn't have had to be all the way on top of the extinct volcano's seventeen-mile height to be unreachable. Surrounding the base of the mountain was a cliff. Compared to seventeen miles of altitude, the cliff wasn't much, only two and a half to three and a half miles tall. Compared to the size of a person it was quite another matter.

Large sections of Olympus Mons were covered by ancient lava flows, and there were significant sections of the cliff that had been smoothed out when the lava splashed and spilled over its edge. Someday they would want to explore the region. It wouldn't be easy going by any means, but it was at least possible. It would mean traversing very rough terrain, though, and using mountain-climbing techniques such as ropes and pitons and crampons. There would be a constant danger of landslides. People might do it, but their rovers? No way. And there would certainly be no chance of bringing back a substantial cargo.

But at least they didn't have to worry about *that*

problem. The pod was on the Tharsis bulge, not Olympus Mons. Even so, that was far enough that it might have well been on another planet entirely.

Not that people weren't running lots of strange ideas through the computers. One woman had the idea of setting the pod on its side and rolling it down the bulge and across the desert. It was like a mountain, right, and things roll off mountains, don't they? As mountains go, though, the Tharsis bulge was more of a gentle hill; if you were standing on it you'd think it was pretty flat, with a slight hint of incline. It was so big because it went on for such a great distance. The pod, however, had never been built for being tipped on its side and turned around and around for tens of thousands of turns. So rolling didn't look like a real great idea after all.

Resupply from Earth was another option. With the requirements of orbits and propulsion systems, and the lag time on Earth of pulling together another shipment and sending it off, another pod wouldn't arrive for another two years. Earth was moving to do it anyway. They were frustrated, too, and wanted to help out, but launching a new pod for delivery in two years was unfortunately the only concrete step open to them. It was frustrating and it was unfortunate because the crew of *Santa Maria* would be getting pretty hungry by the time the resupply pod arrived, no one had any doubt about that. Still, that wasn't exactly the *only* other option. There were still the other two bases, around the *Pinta* and *Niña*.

133

They *were* the *Santa Maria* base's only neighbors, after all. *Niña* and *Pinta* weren't exactly right next door, but considering that the three of them were the only settlements on the entire planet, Nathan was willing to be a little loose about his definition for what "next door" might really mean under the circumstances. *Niña* had come in about ten miles southwest of *Santa Maria*'s landing site and *Pinta* was another ten miles farther west and fifteen miles or so to the north, so that the three ships had landed in a rough and stretched-out triangle. The idea had been to set them down far enough away from each other that a calamity at one site wouldn't take down everyone, but close enough so they could support each other to a limited extent if it became necessary. In addition, once the settlements had been stabilized, they could set up regular traffic and interchange between themselves.

Unhappily, the planners had considered the chances of such a serious combination of problems to be very slim, and they hadn't figured on one base needing a wholesale bailout from the others. Actually, the problem was even worse than that. *Niña* had lost one of her three pods when its parachute had come out tangled and the pod had plunged straight into the ground ten miles from the ship without braking at all. As a result, *Niña*'s base was on the same restricted-supply planning that *Santa Maria*'s had been before the greenhouse blowout. *Pinta* was doing better, but *Pinta* was even farther away. They could run supply convoys to *Pinta*, and people on both ships were busily analyzing and planning just that thing, but the logistics involved in transporting as much stuff as *Santa Maria* would need were going to represent a major strain on everyone concerned. Even at that, the only "trucks" they had available were the rovers. The rovers would have to go on full-time hauling duty in order to balance their limited capacity, and they'd have to hope none of them broke down.

"It's all my fault," Karl announced. He'd had plopped himself down in a niche of The Commons with the rest of his group. They were *all* tired and the frustration and strain they were under hadn't helped at all.

"It's old news, Karl," said Nathan.

"If I had landed the pod properly none of this would have happened. Well, I mean *some* of it would have happened, but we wouldn't be in such a bad position."

"All right," Lanie said, her eyes closed, propped up against the round sofa in front of Nathan and Sergei. "It's all your fault. You want it, you got it. Now either fix it or shut up about it."

Karl started to steam. "From my first day in this team—"

"Enough," Gen interrupted. "Can it, dude. Nobody's going to start a fight with you, so stop trying to pick one."

"Stop picking on me!"

"You are picking on yourself," Sergei pointed out.

"I should just get in the rover and drive to the

pod. I could make it there, I'm—"

"—the best driver," said Sergei. "Yes, we know all about that."

"But we know the pod's in reasonably good condition! We got hi-res pictures from the satellite."

"How are you going to get there?" Nathan said. "There's a lot of rough terrain on the way, isn't there? Then even if you can open the pod up and unpack it, how are you going to bring back enough stuff to make it worthwhile?"

"That is why someone has to go and find out. If I'd even just set the thing down with some fuel remaining . . ." Karl muttered. Then he fell silent.

"Yeah?" said Nathan. "Finish your thought. What then?"

Karl stuck out his jaw belligerently at the ceiling. "If it had fuel left, I bet I could blast the pod off and *fly* it over here."

Half their heads swiveled to look at Karl, then swiveled in unison to look at Noemi. She was chewing on a fingernail. Then, realizing all at once what she'd been up to, she hurriedly pulled her finger out of her mouth and sat on her hand. "Yes, Ms. Math?" Sergei said. "Could Karl do that?"

Noemi shrugged, her eyes going blank for a moment in contemplation. "Maybe," she said. "Perhaps. The Martian gravity is low, the pod is higher up, the atmosphere is thinner up there, too, it shouldn't need as much thrust. A suborbital hop with powered braking at the end? I don't know how much the pod masses. The pod is already five miles up;

that would cut down on the propulsion requirements. And the fuel. Possibly." She shrugged again.
"It's only hypothetical. There *isn't* any fuel."

"Wait a minute," said Gen. His own eyes were
unfocused. But they had started to gleam, and
sweat was breaking out on his forehead. "Wait a
*minute!* All we need is fuel?"

" 'All,' he says," Karl spat morosely. "Yes, that's
'all.' "

"But we've *got* fuel!" Gen announced. "I mean, we
can *make* fuel!"

They all gaped at him. Then Karl's expression
turned to a scowl. "Not another one of your jokes,
please."

"No, *really*," said Gen. "I—"

"Of course!" Sergei shouted suddenly. "Hydrazine!
And nitrogen tetroxide, right?"

Everyone shifted their dropped jaws and aston-
ished expressions to him. He was too excited to
care. "Synthetic pathways, right? The atmosphere
miner, the raw materials—nitrogen! Or were you
thinking of liquid oxygen?"

Gen shook his head. "Too much work, probably
have to redo the plumbing on the pod's engine if we
switch to another kind of fuel. With the materials
we've already built up—"

"Will someone please tell me what's going on
here?" said Alice.

"The engines were fueled with hydrazine," said
Gen, "a standard liquid propellant used in thousands of launches back to the dawn of the space

137

age. You can make hydrazine from ammonia, and we're *already* making ammonia. We've already got a tank of it outside!"

"Let's run the figures," Nathan said. "And then I think we'd better tell somebody about this."

# Chapter Thirteen

"I don't know about this," said Dr. Allen.

Nathan was sitting across the desk from her. The conference screen still showed various overlapping windows highlighting the different features of the plan Nathan and his team had worked out — maps, the travel plan, lists of equipment to be loaded, resource consumption curves showing the amount of air, water, and other supplies that would have to be brought along. The window on top showed the flight trajectory Lanie and Noemi had calculated on the computer. "The calculations say it could work," Nathan said cautiously.

As team leader, he'd been the one elected to present the plan to Dr. Allen. They had spent a while discussing whether or not they should all go in to see Dr. Allen together, but then someone — Nathan thought it had probably been his pal Sergei — had asked what they had a team leader *for*, if not to lead them in situations like this. So it had been Nathan doing a solo, again.

Not that he minded, at least not that much. Nathan wanted to do his part, too. He'd felt left out during the rapid-fire discussion while they'd been working out the details. His knowledge was pretty broad and he wasn't exactly a dope himself. Each of the members of his team, though, had spent a lot of time and effort on expanding their own individual abilities and gifts. With the education and training they now had, any of them could have held their own against a university professor in their chosen topic, or at least against a talented graduate student. Compared to them, Nathan sometimes wanted to fade into a corner and keep his mouth shut.

He had to keep reminding himself that his job wasn't to equal them in their depth of knowledge. Nathan's job was to ride herd on his gang, to steer them and channel them when necessary, to point them at a problem, let them loose, and get out of the way. And to serve as their spokesman. "We wouldn't propose this lightly," Nathan went on. "None of us want to kill ourselves."

"This is risky," Dr. Allen stated. "You know that. This is very risky."

"In that other talk we had . . ."

"Yes," said Dr. Allen. "I know what I said. There will be times when we may *have* to take risks. I thought we'd already looked at every option, but you people certainly came up with a new one. You seem to have done your homework, too. Even so,

I'm going to want to see everything checked by others."

They had expected that. Why not? It was a good idea, and it *would* be their own necks on the line. They didn't want to set out having missed something important. "Sounds good to us," Nathan told her.

"Hmm," she said. "Yes. You and your team think you're the ones who should actually *do* this mission, I take it."

"Well, ah," said Nathan. "Yes, we do. We thought of it, we worked it out, and we're willing to take the risk. It wouldn't be right to plan a stunt like this and then make somebody else carry it out. I mean, we don't want to hog all the fun. Not all of us need to go, and we should have Ian McShane with us to handle any repairs, but, yeah, we don't want to get shut out. We want to do this."

"Okay. If your plan still looks good after the checking is done, your people have got it."

"All right!" Nathan said to himself. His face must have showed it, or maybe he'd even murmured it out loud, since Dr. Allen broke out with an amused smile of her own.

"Well," she said, scrutinizing him, "if you're going to set out to cross trackless wastes on a dangerous mission, one critical item of equipment surely has to be a feeling of enthusiasm. Right?"

"Uh, yeah," said Nathan. "I was just thinking the same thing."

It was true. The plan had given his team new energy. Even Karl had roused himself from his funk at the idea of having a second chance at the pod he felt so guilty for losing. Karl wasn't one hundred percent happy, but then Nathan wasn't sure he'd ever seen him that way, except perhaps when he was going full speed on some really difficult piloting task. Karl's remaining problem this time was that he couldn't be in two places at once. As the best driver on the expedition, he wanted to be the one at the controls of the rover on the way to the pod. The controls for the pod, however, were back on *Santa Maria*. He was not about to let anyone else pilot "his" pod back to the ship, even if they could possibly manage it. Not that anyone else could, of course, but the only person who was going to have that chance was himself. So Karl would have to stay behind.

Karl and Ian were tight these days, though, after initially trying to pulverize each other back in the "old days" in space after their departure from Earth. If Karl wasn't going, the next best thing was that his pal Ian was.

Most everyone else in Nathan's team was going too, however. Sergei would be the principal driver. He wasn't quite in Karl's league, but he was good.

The backup driver was Noemi. Back on Earth, to discover Noemi's own level of skill with motor vehicles had been a bit of a surprise, even though it really shouldn't have been. One of the things Noemi had been happy to shop for had been a car, and her family had been perfectly happy for their part to provide her with one. She hadn't been inhibited by any thought of treating the car gently, of course. If it wore out they'd just get a new one. In the process of working out her initial wildness she'd also built up a solid, comprehensive set of driving talents. The advanced driving class she'd attended at a raceway, taught by a retired Formula One winner and antiterrorist consultant, hadn't hurt any, either.

Gen was along to superintend the miner, finish brewing the porpellant, and refuel the pod's tanks. He and Ian would deal with any other mechanical problems that might crop up. Someone might need to hit the computer intensively at some point, so that meant Lanie was in as well, and Nathan had included himself because there was no possible way anyone was going to leave him out. If nothing else, he'd be an extra pair of arms.

A team of six people was the maximum the single rover could transport, along with enough supplies to sustain them and the stuff they'd need to do the job once they'd arrived. They'd dismissed the idea of bringing both rovers as soon as it had come up; they only had two, and the base certainly needed at least one on-site. If the expedition to the pod ran into serious trouble, the second rover could serve as a rescue vehicle as well. Unfortunately, one of the pieces of equipment the base was lacking was a vehicle designed for long-distance trips. A follow-up cargo shipment from Earth in the next few years was scheduled to deliver a more elaborate vehicle that was really more of a mobile home. With a pressurized interior and its own airlock, people would be able to work inside the vehicle without space suits and generally travel in a lot more comfort on trips that could be as much as a month long and range hundreds or thousands of miles. This vehicle would probably weigh five or ten tons on Earth, though, so the problem of fitting it into a Mars shipment wasn't easy, especially when people had to eat and breathe and so forth first. The dune buggy rover wouldn't be comfortable and it wouldn't make things easy, but, on the other hand, they actually had it available.

Even if they could have fit more people into the expedition, Alice wouldn't have been one of them. The task of getting the greenhouse back in operation and hopefully salvaging something of the seeds and sprouts demanded her skills and her special touch. "You guys better watch out for yourselves," she told Nathan at daybreak three days after his talk with Dr. Allen. "I don't want to be part of a two-person team."

"Six of us are going, and six of us are coming back," Nathan promised. None the worse for wear, he hoped. Behind him, one of the rovers had already been backed out of its garage and was getting its final checkout. Attached to the rover's trailer hitch was a veritable train of supplies, air tanks, collapsed tents, water bags, and containers full of the raw constituents of rocket fuel. When it came right down to it, the expedition hadn't taken that long to plan and assemble. Of course, it had become the job with the highest priority around, first when its bare feasibility was being checked and then later when they were getting down to the task of making it all work.

Karl joined them. He was visibly nervous, probably even more so than the ones who were going, Nathan thought. That was certainly the reason — Karl would be on the sidelines for days yet with no way to take a direct role. "Don't screw this up," he told Nathan. "I want my chance with that pod."

"And you'll get it. Don't worry."

"I know," Karl said. "I know. I . . . I'm going inside." He went back toward the airlock.

"Ignore him," Alice said. "You'll do great."

"Nathan!" came Sergei's voice. "Time to go!"

"I'm coming," said Nathan. He looked at Alice. "Well, you heard the man," he said tentatively.

Alice moved close and hugged him briefly. "Good luck," she said. "You won't need it and it's so . . . so *trite* to mention it, but what the heck. It can't hurt, can it?"

"Nope," said Nathan. "Gotta go." That was about all he thought he could handle saying right at the moment. If his gang was like family, Alice was like the sister he'd never had. It was good she wasn't, like, his girlfriend; that would be pretty heavy. Alice knew him too well.

But Lisette hadn't come to see him off. Nathan knew her work schedule was tight, but so was Alice's, and *she'd* managed to come. Things had been so hectic for everyone since they'd landed and

145

they'd all been so exhausted all the time that every-thing in life except work and sleep had seemed to fade away. It suddenly hit Nathan how he hadn't said more than a greeting in passing to Lisette in probably two weeks. At best, they were coasting. And she hadn't come to see him off. He'd have to find out his status when he got back.

Nathan moved back, and then turned and headed for the rover. The sun had cleared the horizon. It *was* time to go.

Around him, everyone was fastening their safety belts — Sergei and Nathan in the front, Noemi and Lanie in the second set of regular seats, and Gen and Ian in the extra seats rigged out over the first module, one with its own direct-drive motors to help drag the load. Nathan patted Sergei on the shoulder and gave him a thumbs-up. The others chimed in with their systems checks. Sergei engaged the motor and set them on the road.

"I've got this feeling of déjà vu," said Nathan. "Why does it feel like we've done this before?"

"Because we *have* done this before," Sergei reminded him. "Only that time it rained."

It was true. Their graduation exercise from the training program in Houston had been a survival trek in the desert. The team had designed their own lightweight dune buggy to ride them out of that one. Nathan had thought then that the Texas out-back was more empty and rugged than Mars could possibly be, but of course he hadn't seen Mars yet at that point, either.

"At least we don't have to worry about Suki Long this time," Nathan commented. Suki had been after Nathan's team from the first day they'd met each other back in Houston. Nathan was pretty surprised she'd actually been permitted to go to Mars with the rest of the group with an attitude like hers. It wasn't just attitude, either. She'd been the one who'd arranged the sabotage of their other vehicle on the Texas desert.

"Haven't you noticed everybody's more serious since we landed? Being on the ground here makes it all real. It's not a game, it's not Suki Long against everyone else. It's all of us together against the planet. Is that not so?" Sergei said.

No one had anything to say to that, or maybe they were just being charitable toward Suki, Nathan thought. He sure agreed with Sergei. This was real, not some test. Wherever you looked, it just underlined the point. He gazed off to the side across the morning landscape with its sharp shadows and tufts of ground fog. There was, of course, the horizon, which was far too close, the sky, which was far too pink, and the gravity, which was far too weak. No, not a test by any means.

"Perhaps it is finally a good omen," Gen said after a while. "Our experience on the survival trek, I mean."

"Yeah," said Lanie. "You're right."

Back then, if the team had failed, they might have lost their chance to go to Mars. This time, though, their failure might cost them their very lives, and could endanger the lives of all their companions.

Nathan felt a nudge in his side.

"Cheer up," Sergei told him. "We are off to a good start. Save your worrying for later — that's when you really may need it."

# Chapter Fourteen

Driving through most of the daylight hours, stopping only to change drivers and give everybody a quick stretch-out break, they crossed a lot of the same type of terrain they'd already grown familiar with around the landing site. Not only had they gotten familiar with the way it looked, Sergei and Noemi had had ample chance to learn the peculiarities of driving across it. For short jaunts in the vicinity of the base they had kept their driving speed down to twenty miles an hour or so. Now, though, they had a lot of ground to cover. And their air and other supplies were not unlimited. So Sergei and Noemi were trying to push the driving pace as much as they could and still try to be safe. It wouldn't help them if they shaved two days off their travel time and then got stuck in a ditch, or worst of all, wrecked the rover.

Still, when they stopped for the first night in the midst of a long field scattered with small rocks, their wheel tracks loping backward behind them to the horizon, Sergei announced that they had covered close to three hundred miles. "We were driving fairly much due east, too," Sergei added. "Most of the distance we traveled is actually straight toward our goal."

The satellite confirmed their progress. "You're looking good, Nathan," said Karl, his voice relayed from *Santa Maria* to the satellite to the expedition. "Just on the predicted track. You are already in the record books—farthest trek on another planet, greatest distance away from base."

"What else did you expect?" Nathan responded. "We're good."

Signing off, he went to join the others, who had begun setting up the tent.

"Can we really fit six people in this thing?" Noemi was saying.

"It's either this or the bags," Sergei reminded them.

"At least we'll be able to get out of these suits," said Noemi.

"What are you complaining about?" Lanie said. "You were happier than any of us to get these suits in the first place."

Noemi said something that sounded pointed back to her, but it was in Spanish, which none of the others present knew.

Lanie hmphed into her throat mike and turned away to smooth the closest corner of the tent. She wasn't mad at Noemi, not really, she just got a little exasperated with her from time to time. Not that it was her fault she'd been born with those looks, or that no matter what she ate her figure couldn't care less, or that she could twist a guy around her finger almost in her sleep if she had a mind to. Lanie liked Noemi. She couldn't help being what she was any more than Lanie could help being who she was.

Back on Earth she'd been just another kid from the housing projects in the bad side of a nowhere town. Here on Mars, and through the training and the trip, she'd remade herself. *Stand tall, girl,* she told herself. *You've earned it.* But so had Noemi. She was a different person, too. So were all of them, to one extent or another. "You guys are all right," she said out loud, forgetting to turn off her microphone so she could mumble to herself.

She didn't realize she'd spoken for everybody to hear until she felt a hand on her shoulder. "Noemi. I'm glad you're here," she said softly. "I'm glad you're all here. This is a bad place to be with no friends, I think."

"Check this out," Gen said brightly. "There's more land area on Mars than there is on Earth. Earth's bigger, but three-quarters of the surface is ocean."

"I don't know about you guys," said Nathan, "but I'm ready to head in. How about it?"

They all agreed with him. The sun had set while they were working, and it was cooling off rapidly. One after another the six explorers ducked through

151

the low entranceway into the shelter. The walls were more of that flimsy-looking plastic that half their gear seemed to be made out of, with another zipper-and-sealstrip arrangement to close it off from the outside. When they were all inside sprawled together on the floor, Nathan closed up the doorway behind them and triggered the airtank. They could all hear the hissing as the tent began to fill with air, and the plastic walls started to tense as the pressure built up against them.

"That's it until morning," Nathan said. "I hope nobody forgot anything outside." The shelter was too small for an airlock. It was designed to be pumped up when everyone was inside and deflated when it was time to get out.

"Have the seals on this thing been tested?" asked Sergei. "I do not worry, as you know, but still I am wondering just a little."

"I inflated it myself yesterday," said Ian. "Everything checked out, and the satellites report no dust storms anywhere in sight."

"Who brought the marshmallows?" Gen said.

"Marshmallows? Whatever are you talking about?" said Sergei.

"It's American," Gen explained, his face perfectly straight and serious. "Whenever these American dudes are camping out they make a campfire and roast marshmallows over it. On coathangers. I hope none of you dudes forgot your coathangers."

"You've got to be kidding," groaned Lanie.

"Didn't you ever build a campfire and roast things over it?" said Gen, his expression still guileless behind his helmet visor.

"In my neighborhood kids roasted *cars*. At least when they were *kids*, before they graduated to bigger things."

"In *my* neighborhood . . ." Ian began.

"Ah," said Gen. "I see. Sorry. We must go back to the ship."

"Why?" Nathan said. "To get your marshmallows? The closest marshmallows are about fifty million miles away."

"No, to trade you and Lanie for some real Americans. You must have cleverly infiltrated our group in disguise, but you are clearly not genuine Americans. All Americans know about campfires and marshmallows." He looked seriously back at Nathan. Then all at once Gen finally lost it. He cracked a small smile in the corner of his mouth, but then it quickly spread to envelop his whole face. "Gotcha, dude!"

"Perhaps it is the air here," said Sergei thoughtfully. "Something is clearly affecting his mind."

"It says the pressure is normal and holding," Noemi commented, cracking the seal on her helmet. A moment later they had all removed their helmets and peeled out of their suits. Underneath they'd been wearing a mixture of shorts and T-shirts and regulation coveralls.

"Keep your gear close at hand," warned Nathan.

153

"The alarm will sound if we start to lose pressure, but if there's a problem we may only have a few seconds."

"Affirmative, Captain," said Gen.

"Where else *can* we put our gear?" said Sergei.

It was true. Their tent wasn't what you could call spacious. You couldn't even stand up, and the six of them were crammed in almost on top of each other, but at least they were in from the outside.

"Enough of this," Lanie said. "Who brought the pizza?"

Dinner wasn't nearly as interesting as a good old thick pizza with onion and pineapple, Lanie's favorite, might have been. Nobody had been expecting it to be, of course. You weren't supposed to have catered food on a genuine adventure, though, Nathan thought. If this wasn't a genuine adventure he didn't know what was.


Guided by the computer maps and the satellite reconnaissance, they stayed ahead of their schedule for the next two days, camping at night in their tent and making tracks while the sun was up. Gradually and almost imperceptibly the ground had been rising ever since they'd left the base. Where the *Santa Maria* had landed, the surface was a little over a mile above "sea level," which on Mars didn't mean anything about the presence of water, of course, just the standard reference ground plane. Now they

154

were already more than two miles higher than they'd started as they ascended the long Tharsis bulge. They still had some serious ground to travel, though. The ground there was still pretty smooth, but Cargo Pod Two's location was almost six miles above sea level.

When it hit them midway on their fourth day of travel, though, the problem had very little to do with the terrain or the altitude at all, although the altitude and the terrain did make it worse. Even without the added factors it was bad enough all by itself.

"Nathan!" Karl's voice suddenly rang out over the hailing channel they always kept open for communication with the base. "Come in!"

A lot of static on the line, Nathan thought absently as he flipped his channel selection to allow him to transmit as well as listen. "Nathan here, Karl. What's up?"

"There's a solar flare building, a big one," Karl said. "They picked it up on Earth and radioed immediately. The radiation—" Static interrupted the transmission.

"What was that?" said Nathan. He was sitting in the backseat behind Noemi, who was the driver at the moment. "I didn't copy. Your transmission sounds like it's breaking up."

"It will do more than this," Karl said into a moment of sudden calm. "The early radiation from the flare is already starting to arrive. You will probably

155

lose contact entirely with the ship and the satellite within half an hour, but—"

"Say again, Karl." Nathan switched the other four in on the same communications circuit. "We're going to have to get under cover quick, team. There's a big solar flare on the way."

*"Bozhe moi!"* That had to be Sergei. All of them, however, knew from their basic class in Things That Could Kill You On Mars just what they were facing. Every so often, the Sun, which was basically a titanic nuclear reactor running out of control for ten billion years or so, would send out an extra explosion of charged atomic particles—a solar flare. The detonation of an Earth-made atomic weapon was nothing compared to what the Sun itself could put out. A single flare could release the energy of ten million thermonuclear bombs in the space of a few minutes.

There was a lot of space for that energy to spread out to cover as it slammed out across the solar system, but there was a lot of energy, too. How the radiation from a flare could disrupt communications all over Earth had been understood for years. What scientists also understood was the role that the Earth's magnetic field played in shielding the planet from dangerous effects. No one had had a chance to test the effects on Mars.

Until now.

Suddenly Karl was back. "They expect the most dangerous radiation to start arriving here in an

156

hour. You must get under cover immediately! Everyone here is retreating to the storm shelters already." The ships had been built with a central area shielded by the water tanks. If they were caught by a flare while still in space, the crew could hide in this storm shelter while the water absorbed the dangerous particles. On the ground, they had already built their underground shelters, covered by several feet of Martian dirt.

That was fine for the folks back at the base, but it wouldn't help the six explorers now. They didn't have enough water to hide under and they didn't have enough time to dig foxholes with their shovels. "We haven't passed any caves," said Lanie. Noemi had pulled the vehicle to a halt. They were in a field of boulders and loose dirt; a shallow ravine lay just ahead. A cave, though, was what really would have been useful, but Lanie was right. They hadn't seen anything like a cave all day.

Karl was gone again. "Dirt," said Nathan, thinking as hard as he could. They were *all* thinking as hard as they could. "We've got plenty of dirt, but we've only got an hour, max. Anybody with an idea just speak up."

"I know what we can do," Sergei said slowly. "But you won't like it. It will only work for five of us."

# Chapter Fifteen

Sergei was right, Nathan didn't like it. Unfortunately they didn't have a whole lot of choice in the matter, since it was the best idea any of them was able to think of in the next minute, and it had the advantage that it would probably work. For five of them.

"It is my idea," Sergei said. "I am also the driver; that means I am the best qualified to do this job. I am the most expendable — my skills are the ones least necessary to rescuing the pod. I should be the one to stay out."

"What are you now," Nathan said helplessly, "a martyr?"

"No. I would welcome a better idea, but time is running out."

Unfortunately, what Sergei had said was not entirely true. "If anyone's expendable," said Nathan, "it's not you. It's me."

"Even so," Sergei said with a devil-may-care grin,

"I have the car keys. I will not negotiate."

*Sergei's my best friend,* Nathan thought. But they only had minutes. No time to argue. "Let's get on it," he said.

"Wait," said Ian. "Wait! There *is* another way, you idiots. We do it like this . . ."


They got on it. It was one thing to discuss Sergei's idea with Ian's modification in the abstract, though, and quite another thing to put it into practice. For the five of them to sit up against the wall of the depression in the survival tent while Sergei headed toward them in the rover, its bulldozer blade lowered, was enough to freak you out more than a little bit, but that wasn't the half of it. When the bulldozer started actually pushing dirt over the edge of the ravine right on top of their heads—well, that was enough to make even the most non-neurotic person get at least a twinge of claustrophobia.

"Buried alive, dudes," Gen said nervously, looking up through his helmet screen at red dirt. A few sunlit patches still showed off on the sides where the dirt had not yet covered them. Sunlight. At the moment, that very sunlight was their biggest enemy. Wherever the light was falling, the radiation from the solar flare would soon follow.

They were past the maximum point in the eleven-year sunspot cycle, which meant that they were past the peak of flare danger, too, since flare activity went along with sunspots. This wasn't the first encounter the Mars expedition had had with the harmful potential of the sun; their other experience had been all the way back in Earth orbit. "I don't think I'll ever be able to go out in the sun again without getting scared," Noemi admitted. "You never see any of these dangers back in Venezuela."

"We're not in Kansas now," commented Gen.

"Kansas?" said Noemi. "Who said anything about Kansas?"

*I lived in the United States all my life,* Nathan thought, *and here's this guy from Japan quoting* The Wizard of Oz. *Well, that's the way things go.*

The barrage of dirt stopped and the rumble of the rover drew to a halt. In the ravine next to the tent, they'd propped up some of the supplies from the trailer to make a small space that kept the dirt in that area from falling all the way to the ravine's floor. Laid out in this narrow space was one of the one-person survival cocoons. Nathan realized he was holding his breath waiting to hear from Sergei.

Legs first, Sergei slid himself backward down the passageway, his shoulders barely clearing the entranceway. His chest and his backpack were both scraping along opposite surfaces. It was a tight fit. Squirming like a snake, he fitted himself into the survival bag.

As he'd moved into the bag, Sergei had taken hold of a rope they'd tied to the plate that was holding the dirt off the first few feet of the tunnel.

Now he yanked forcefully on it. The plate broke loose and came toward him. With its support removed, the end of the tunnel collapsed, gently shaking the ravine and covering Sergei with dirt.

"Nathan, I am underground," Sergei radioed.

They were under cover. *All* of them. "Roger, Sergei. Thanks to Ian."

"I wasn't going to leave one of my mates outside to glow in the dark," said Ian, "now was I? Just another spot of teamwork. Now I don't know about the rest of you, but I'm for a nap. Isn't nothing to do but wait anyway."

That was a good enough idea for all of them. That is, if they could calm down enough to catch some sleep.

"What was that?" Nathan said muzzily. He'd left the com channel on his radio turned on with the volume turned part way down, but all he'd been hearing was the white noise of static. They'd left an antenna wire stretched out along the ravine so they could hear if anyone was able to contact them, but surely it was far too soon to expect that. What time was it, anyway? The last time he'd been up had been early evening . . .

Much to his surprise, it was already the next morning. Still, the thought that he'd heard a voice through the static had to be his imagin—

"Nathan! Pod team, come in!"

It wasn't his mind playing tricks! "Karl? Nathan here!"

He heard a distant cheer. There must be a roomful of people surrounding Karl back at the *Santa Maria* com board. Karl muttered something in German, then, in English, said, "Thank God. The flare was a small one and radiation levels are dropping rapidly. Are all of you . . ."

By this time everyone in the tent was up, too. They all let out a roar of their own. "You hear that?" Nathan shouted over the din. "That's your answer!"

After a few minutes of comparing notes and getting the latest updates on the situation, it was apparent that the danger had passed. "What are we waiting for?" said Lanie. "Let's get ourselves out of here and get our act back on the road!"

# Chapter Sixteen

It was the afternoon of the day after Nathan's group had dug themselves out of their emergency shelter and had resumed their trek toward their destination. As they had climbed higher and higher, the horizon had pulled back and the distance they could see expanded. "Still just a lot of empty sand and rocks if you ask me," Noemi said. She was taking her turn in the driver's seat. "This place needs a good decorator."

Sergei was next to her in the front seat, scanning the area ahead of them with a pair of binoculars. "It's not quite all sand and rocks," he stated after a moment.

It took a moment for Sergei's comment to sink in. "Can you see it?" asked Nathan. He had another binocular trained on the scene, too, but he was willing to admit that Sergei's eyesight was sharper than his own.

"There," said Sergei, pointing just a bit to the

163

right of their current heading. The cargo pod had a location beeper that they'd turned on as they neared its site, and that had guided their steering along with the orbital maps. Still, it was one thing to know the pod was there because it was beeping and quite another to get it in their visual sights. "Do you see?"

There was the tilted plain, the usual small rocks, the red dirt, the pink sky, and—a regular conical shape! It was the pod.

It took them another half hour to reach the landing site. When they had parked, though, the six of them almost piled over each other in their eagerness to get out and get to work. Each person knew their tasks. Gen got to work setting up the refinery apparatus on the tanks of fuel ingredients they'd brought with them. Ian, assisted by Sergei and Nathan, had to get into the engine compartment and check to see what repairs or tuning up might be needed. Lanie and Noemi were to inspect the remainder of the pod's exterior, comparing what they could see and probe for with the specifications in the computer.

Late that night, working under lamps, they got together to review their findings. Karl and the home team sat in over their com link. "The big question, team," Nathan said, "is, can we do it? Ian?"

"There's a spot of work to do on that fuel valve that gave Karl such a rough time. The engine nozzle's rather a bit fried, too, but it should hold out for the length of the trip we're talking about here. There's a few more odds and ends to tighten up on, but the engine should do the job. Tomorrow afternoon, say four o'clock."

"That quick?" said Karl. "Wonderful!"

*He's dancing back there,* Nathan thought. "Gen? How about the fuel situation?"

"Well, dude, it's like this: I'll be ready to pump when Ian's finished with his motors."

"What?" said Nathan. "I thought it would take four or five days to finish refining the fuel!"

"How long have we been on the road?"

"You were running the refining system while we were driving?" said Sergei. "You were making rocket fuel while we were bouncing over rocks? You could have blown us up!"

"Chill out, man," Gen told him. "I didn't want to get you worried. I ran the simulations, I checked it out. It was pretty safe."

"Pretty safe!" Sergei groaned. "This is the last time I'm going on a job with you, you maniac."

"Hey, it worked out, all right? But if we can start pumping at four we should be tanked up by the middle of the evening. Then it's flight checks from Karl and Ian, right? Should be ready to lift off at dawn."

"Let's not get ahead of things," Nathan cautioned. "Lanie? What about your inspection?"

"Well, these pods are only built to land once and then stay where they land," said Lanie. "There's no real way of telling how well one will hold together on a second flight. I'm kind of worried about one of the landing legs. I noticed it's got a crack starting. All we can do is try and see what happens, I guess. Karl? You better bring this thing in with a soft touch."

"It's risky, but then we knew that when we started out," Nathan summed up. "We're here to do a job and we're going to do it!"

Fortunately they'd gotten some extra sleep and rest while hiding from the solar flare, because now the six of them plunged into the challenge before them with full force, snatching only a few hours' sleep in the deep of the night. Their suit heaters were turned up to maximum, but it was still chilly. There were reasons why people hadn't wanted to work outside after the sun went down. The sooner they were finished here, though, the sooner their friends might be able to get the pod's much-needed supplies.

Then it was daytime, and the work continued. Lanie, Nathan, and Noemi opened some of the pod's access hatches to check the conditions of the supplies packed inside. Some of the restraints had actually come loose during the pod's eventful descent, and it took a while to resettle them. Gen watched his fuel apparatus like a mother hen with a prime clutch of eggs. His habitual cool was there, but if you knew Gen you could tell it was more strained than usual. Ian clambered around the engine, contorting himself through panels and around pipes and ducts with various wrenches and screwdrivers and electrical test apparatus in his hands. Right on schedule, though, he pronounced himself satisfied. They hooked up the fuel lines and carefully started the pumps.

Night came again. From *Santa Maria,* Dr. Allen and Karl established their full-scale communications link with the pod and began testing the flight systems. This time, of course, they had a mechanic on site, and they found enough things to be adjusted to keep Ian tinkering much of the night. The others napped in shifts. Everyone was getting pretty exhausted, but at the same time they were keyed up with expectation. It seemed as though morning would never arrive, but of course it did.

The rover was repacked. The pod was refueled. Its systems were tested and retested. The computer simulations were right on the mark. "The only thing left is to do it," Nathan said. "Time to move out."

The team climbed into the rover and Noemi drove them down the slope away from the pod, poised expectantly in the early-morning light. She stopped a mile away to keep them clear of the blast from the pod's engine, or from debris if the worst happened and the pod exploded on launch. Ian and Gen stayed behind until the last moment, ready to run for shelter behind several huge boulders. Over the com link they could hear Karl and Dr. Allen beginning the final part of their countdown.

"Here we are again," Karl muttered. He could do it; he knew he could do it. Still, he kept noticing that his palms were wet, and that he was compulsively clenching and loosening his fists.

"If you keep doing that, you may wear them out," said Dr. Allen, trying to ease the boy's tension.

"Will I?" he asked nervously, stretching his hands out flat on his legs by an effort of will.

"Probably not, actually," she said with a small smile. Karl thought she was nervous, too.

They had enough to be nervous about. This was a maneuver no one had ever done before. The flight instructions Karl and Dr. Allen had created had been loaded into the computers, but there was no way to program the emergency maneuvers that might be necessary. They were dealing with a used pod, after all. Who knew what it would do after it left the ground?

"One minute and counting," Karl said. Whether things went perfectly or badly, it would be a short flight. It would be measured in minutes. Only a small hop compared to the distance it had already traveled.

Ten seconds, and then even those melted away. Karl and Dr. Allen had their hands on their individual controls. Two, one, zero. Ignition!

"It's working!" Karl said over the cheering from his headphones. "Throttling up to 110 percent. It's

168

in the air!"

"Fuel consumption is right on the mark," added Dr. Allen. That would be one of the most important things to watch during the flight. If everything went right, the pod would land with the tanks almost dry. If anything went wrong, well . . . all bets were off. The engine would run continuously throughout the flight, too, first to push the pod up and then to brake it coming down.

The pod was already one mile up, then two. Since it had been over five miles high while it was on the ground, it had started out with that major break, too. "Everything's still working fine," Karl muttered. "Keep it up, thing, just keep it up."

"Coming up on the midpoint roll," called Dr. Allen. This was the pod's major maneuver during the flight, when it would flip itself end over end so that the rocket motor would be pointing ahead of it on the way down. The pod would be at the top of its long parabola.

"Into the roll," Karl said. "Roll completed!" They were halfway there.

Of course, the last part of the flight could be the most dangerous. If something went wrong on the pod's approach to the base, it could plow off course into the greenhouse crater or into *Santa Maria* herself. Karl's hands tightened again on the controls.

"We've acquired the pod on visual," Dr. Allen reported. The telescope and long-range optics had swung into action again, just as they had on the descent of the successful pods all those weeks ago. Soon the pod's own cameras would pick up the base. Yes! Now the most recognizable feature from the air was not *Santa Maria* but rather the reinflated greenhouse dome.

This time the landing site was to the south of *Santa Maria,* beyond the area the expedition had been developing. The greenhouse crater began to slip to the right of the pod's camera view.

Fuel was disappearing faster than it should. Was there a leak somewhere? That balky fuel valve was working fine, though. "Ten seconds to manual control mark," said Dr. Allen.

"Already?" Karl said. They'd made the decision that Karl would perform the final part of the landing himself, manually. Karl's fine touch was probably better than that of the chain of machines in the loop. They'd soon see for sure.

"Two, one. Mark! I've got it."

The controls came to life in his hands. "Softly, softly," Karl murmured. Fuel was down to the last drops, or even fumes—"

The engine cut out.

Karl clenched his teeth as the pod dropped the last few feet. It was on the ground . . . Would the legs hold?

The view tilted. *Santa Maria's* camera showed the pod listing over in the direction of the bad landing leg. That leg had a clear kink where it should have been straight.

But the bottom of the pod was already close to the ground. Then it touched, taking weight off the leg.

The view stabilized. The pod was leaning to one side, but they could deal with that. "Let's get the landing team out there to shore that pod up!" Dr. Allen was calling.

"I hope I never have to do that again," said Karl.

"What?" said Dr. Allen. "That's not the Karl Muller I know. It looked to me like you were having fun."

"A person can only take so much fun," Karl told her.


"Well," Nathan said, "that's that. Mission accomplished."

"I think we deserve a vacation," said Gen, joining the rest of the group with Ian.

"We've got a vacation," Ian said. "A pleasant excursion in the countryside. Starting right now."

The pod might have arrived safely, but their job wasn't over yet. They still had to drive back to the base.

# Chapter Seventeen

The drive had taken six days, but at least that time had been free of major problems. "Home at last," said Lanie. "But where is everybody?"

"It's late," Gen pointed out. "Sun will be down in a few minutes. Everyone's probably inside by now."

"Look at the greenhouse," Nathan said. "It looks good as new. From the outside, anyway."

"No more sightseeing for me," said Noemi. "All I want is a shower, the faster the better."

"There's somebody parked in our garage. Forget it, I'm just too tired to park anyway." He braked to a stop in front of the airlock. "We can put things away in the morning. For now, this is the end of the line."

"I didn't expect a bloody band," said Ian, climbing stiffly out of his seat. "I wouldn't have minded more reception than this lot, though, mates."

It was true, Nathan thought. As if the drive back hadn't been anticlimatic enough, now here they were driving up to a ship that had tucked itself in for the night. He trudged after the others into the airlock.

They went through the usual airlock drill and finally cracked the inner hatch. "Look at this," said Nathan. "They're really letting this place run down. All the lights in the corridor have gone out."

Then the lights came on.

The corridor was packed with people.

"Surprise!" they yelled.

Music was playing. "Let's party!" Gen said, as excited as Nathan had ever heard him.

The six explorers were being mobbed. People were slapping them on the back, shouting congratulations in their ears, hurrying them down the hall, generally letting loose. Sergei had ended up next to Nathan as they entered The Commons. "I don't recognize all these people," he yelled in Nathan's ear. "There must be some people from the other ships here! I wonder if—" He broke off suddenly.

"What?" said Nathan.

"Ludmilla," Sergei said nervously. "Over there."

Sergei's moment of truth had arrived. Nathan watched him head off slowly in her direction. Across the room someone else was waving. At Nathan? Yes, it was Lisette.

But then right there next to him was Alice. She regarded him seriously. "Good job, Nathan," she told him. Then her face broke into a smile, a very wide smile. She shyly put her arms around him and gave him a big hug. "Good job," Alice said again, softly.

Nathan put his arms around Alice, too. "It's good to be back," he said.

LOOK FOR THE YOUNG ASTRONAUTS' NEXT EXCITING SPACE ADVENTURE! THE WHOLE MARS COLONY MUST WORK TO-GETHER TO RESCUE A MISSING COLONIST STRANDED IN THE FROZEN MARTIAN DES-ERT IN—

THE YOUNG ASTRONAUTS #6: CITIZENS OF MARS